P9-DNM-036
OCT 2013

Half the Kingdom

Also by Lore Segal

Shakespeare's Kitchen
Her First American
Lucinella
Other People's Houses

Half the Kingdom

Lore Segal

HALF THE KINGDOM

First Melville House printing: October 2013

Portions of this novel have appeared, in slightly different form, in *The New Yorker* and *Harper's Magazine*.

Melville House Publishing
145 Plymouth Street
Brooklyn, NY 11201

and

8 Blackstock Mews
Islington
London N4 2BT

mhpbooks.com facebook.com/mhpbooks @melvillehouse

Library of Congress
Cataloging-in-Publication Data

Segal, Lore Groszmann.
Half the kingdom : a novel / Lore Segal.
p. cm.
ISBN 978-1-61219-302-1 (hardback)
1. Life change events—Fiction. 2. Psychological fiction. I. Title.
PS3569.E425S44 2013
813'.54—dc23

2013018656

Design by Christopher King

Printed in the United States of America
1 3 5 7 9 10 8 6 4 2

Beatrice Jacob Jean David

Half the Kingdom

And if they have not died, they are living to this hour.
—The Brothers Grimm

I
The Compendium

Joe Bernstine

The doctors, nurses and patients in the overcrowded, too-brightly lit Emergency Room turned toward the commotion. It was the very old woman thrashing about her with improbable strength and agility. "You *do* not," she shouted, "you do *not* tell me to relax! I *will not* relax."

"Is all right, Missis, all right?" said the elderly caregiver as she laid herself across the gurney to help the nurse catch the nonagenarian's flailing legs.

"What did you do with my shoes, Luba, you *do not* take away a person's clothes. Why do you hide my clothes?"

"There she blows," the doctor in the hijab said to the skin-and-bones little patient whose pulse she was taking. "That's our third patient gone berserk in one day. Anstiss Adams is one of our regulars, like you, Mr. —?"

"Bernstine, Joe Bernstine," said the little smiling man.

Dr. Haddad should not have told him, "Our Dr. Stimson

is starting a log of all the sixty-two-pluses who go around the bend."

Bernstine grinned. "Having an Alzheimer's epidemic, are you?"

"Glad to have your diagnosis, Mr. Bernstine."

"Copycat Alzheimer's?" suggested Bernstine, smiling. "Or is there no such a thing?"

If Dr. Haddad relayed this exchange to Dr. Stimson, the Chief of Emergency, it was from the temptation to confess; one should never talk to a patient about other patients. "I asked him what he did, and he said 'I'll be doing my End-of-World Scenarios.' I couldn't tell if he was joking or another one gone around the bend."

"Little Bernstine with the perpetual smile," said Dr. Stimson, looking across the room where the patient's wife had arrived to take him home. "He's been in and out this last month and I've had to tell him that he's terminal. I thought he was going to ask me how long he had to live, but he grinned and said, 'The tree will continue to fall in the forest.' "

Bethy

"What is it with him?" asked Joe Bernstine's daughter, Bethy, some weeks after her father's latest return from Emergency. Joe's wife, Jenny, looked across the breakfast table with her habitual frown of fond anxiety. Joe had just announced renting a two-room office on West 57th Street. "I took over the lease of a dressmakers' establishment that had to close down," Joe said.

"Dear," Jenny said, "wasn't the idea for you to take it easy?"

Joe had retired from the directorship of the Concordance Center, an old and respected Connecticut think tank, soon after 9/11, at a time when his illness had first been diagnosed; he and Jenny had moved back to New York. Now, ten years later, he'd arranged to have lunch with a friend from the company that published the Concordance reports. They had cooked up a project: the definitive history, an encyclopedia, *The Compendium of End-of-World Scenarios*. The question Bethy pitched at her mother hardly differed from the one doctors Haddad and Stimson had asked themselves in the ER: "Is he a clown, or a nut case?" asked Bethy. She belonged to the class of children whose tone of voice is never less than nasty when speaking to parents who continue to respond with incorruptible courtesy.

"I thought," Joe said to her, "this might be a project you'd like to work on with me."

Jenny frowned apologetically at Bethy: The mother was lovelier than the daughter. Jenny's small, racy features had aged handsomely; the hair was stunningly white against the olive of her complexion. On their Italian holiday, Jenny had recognized Bethy's features—the over-ample jowls, the weight of the chin, the hanging cheeks, that little, unhappy mouth—in Piero della Francesca's San Giuliano. Bitter and unfair that the painted saint in the mural was unaccountably beautiful while the daughter who had stood beside her, who sat here, across the table, was a plain woman. Poor Bethy! The diminutive of her given name was not descriptive so much as compensatory.

To her husband, Jenny said, "I don't see how you can go on living ..."

"Go on living?" said Joe.

"In the constant expectation ..."

"Of?" prompted Joe.

Bethy said, "Dad is waiting to get Raptured."

It had made Bethy crazy—her father's addiction to the television ministry of Harold Camping, who preached the imminence of Judgment Day and universal destruction. Bethy had turned the TV off; her father turned it back on, saying, "Wait wait wait! He's going to give us the date!"

The date had come and had gone.

"He spiritually miscalculated, poor Harold," Joe said, "poor old bastard, and then he had a stroke."

"From which you conclude?" Bethy asked him.

" 'That if it be not now, yet it will come.' "

"*What*," shouted Bethy. "What is coming?"

"We wonder why the Jews didn't get out of Europe while the going was possible, but here we stay, in Manhattan."

Benedict

Joe's second hire was Benedict, the son of an old friend, the late Bertie Friedgold. Benedict was one of those men who look like the little boys that they used to be grown unusually large, with a frown.

Benedict chose to speak of "The Definitive Compendium" in quotes. "When we were kids," he told his live-in girlfriend, Gretel, "we used to always draw Uncle Joe Bernstine as a stick-figure person. He needs this office to have his funny ideas in. And to make work for his pain-in-the-ass daughter Bethy."

Gretel, who worked in the Austrian consulate, said, "Yes, and he knew that *you* were looking for a job."

To this Benedict did not have an immediate answer. He said, "All he's had me doing the first week is set up his library of ancient flood literatures, and anything anybody has ever written about meteors, apocalypses, and varieties of doomsdays."

Smiling Joe walked into the back room that Bethy and Benedict shared with the latest hire, Al Lesser, the computer whiz kid from Harvard. Today's funny idea was biological anti-warfare. "Benedict, we'll miss your dad." Bernard Friedgold had been an eminent epidemiologist and Concordance consultant. "Project Head Cold. Line us up experts on the manufacture, storage, transportation, and strategic delivery to each of two sides in their opposing situation rooms, of an epidemic head cold. Both ignorant armies will run out of tissues and want to go to bed, not war!"

Bethy raised her eyes to the heavens above. Al and Benedict continued to regard Joe, who was accustomed to the look in the eyes of interlocutors waiting for the punch line that had already passed them by. He grinned and said, "It was an idea," and returned to his office, but came back to say, "Project Malfunctioning Button. Let's get us some hackers to tamper with The Button so that it will fail to detonate The Bomb."

"*Is* there a button?"

"Shouldn't think so," Joe said, "Therefore put your trust in Murphy: What's supposed to detonate The Bomb may malfunction."

"Da-*ad*!"

Joe handed Bethy a square little fire-red paperback titled *The NO-NONSENSE Guide to* ***TERRORISM***.

Bethy said, "What am I supposed to do with this?"

"You'll contact our old Concordance experts—I'll give you a list—who might contribute articles on attack modes, weapons, targets, sources, goals."

"I think Benedict thinks you're losing it," Bethy said on the way home. Her father considered this and said, "And Benedict may be right."

Joe Bernstine did not expect the irritable Bethy, or the gentle Jenny, or his young Turks in the office to share his fascination with the approaching catastrophe. The sleep that rounded *their* little lives did not have a date; they could not imagine, which is to say that they did not *believe*, in their own end. Joe gave himself credit for having kept an eye on the progress of his illness, and gave credit to the human race that it had been willing, from Ur-times down to our day, to entertain the idea of its own cessation. The logo on the door of the 57th Street office, and at the head of the stationery, was a wide-open eye.

One morning Joe called everyone into his office, which faced 57th Street. He pointed out the window.

Benedict, in the back room, must have been subliminally aware of the wail of the ambulance that was stuck in the traffic of the Seventh Avenue intersection.

"If that had been me in there, that last time," Joe said, "it might have been *my* end-of-world scenario!"

"*Dad!*" Bethy said.

Benedict continued to look out the window. "You want to know something? If that was me in the Toyota, I'd think moving out of the path of the ambulance would get me stuck behind the white SUV without helping the ambulance get around the crosstown bus, and I'd sit tight. That's what people do."

"That," Joe said, "is what people do. Now imagine a midday Midtown attack. No emergency vehicle will get through. The East and West drives will be choked with people who wouldn't know that the bridges have been closed."

Young Al, who had not been brought up on the images in World War II movies, looked to catch Benedict's eye. *What?!*

When the three young people returned to their back room, Al said, "*What* midday Midtown attack!"

"The terrorists are coming! The terrorists are coming!" sang Benedict. Al laughed. Both turned to check that Bethy, in her place at the far side of the room, was out of earshot. She lowered her head.

Al Lesser lowered his voice. "And what's with the everlasting smiley-face?"

"Uncle Joe's antique grin. The smile in the bone."

"What's the new PC for?" Benedict asked Joe.

"I've hired Lucy."

"Joe! Joe, tell me that's a funny joke!" Lucy was Bertie Friedgold's widow and Benedict's mom.

"Until the desk arrives," said Joe, "she can sit at the sewing machine."

No one, so far, had undertaken to research the number to call and have someone pick up the electrified old treadle, the dozen rolls of flowered, striped, and sprigged fabric, and the boxes of spools of snarled colored thread left by the defunct dressmakers' establishment.

"Joe!" cried Benedict. "What does 'The Definitive Compendium' want with a barely e-mail-literate seventy-five-year-old poet with emphysema!"

Joe said, "Did you know it was Concordance that sold Washington on the idea of using the writing community to imagine what the terrorist community might come up with the next time around?"

"Joe, the science fiction community! Mom's literary!"

"She will catalogue and report on contemporary disaster

literature. Which one of you wants to do disaster movies?"

"Not me," said Bethy.

"I will!" said Al.

Benedict asked, "When is she supposed to start?"

"Today," said Joe.

Lucy

That Lucy Friedgold had kept the paper with the address in her hand wasn't—not in Lucy's case—evidence of memory loss. She remembered herself back in her student days and she'd never been able to retain the number in the phone book long enough to dial it.

This was one of her bad-left-leg days, and her cough was troublesome, but Lucy liked 57th Street, full of folk walking west with her, or walking toward her, their eyes inward, talking into their phones.

Lucy liked the funny foyer. It had never been done over. The hazed and spotted mirrors were gold-framed in mail-order rococo. Joe had said to take the back elevator, no longer used for freight, to the eleventh floor.

Behind the door with the emblem of a wide-open eye, they stopped talking to listen to the clank and rasp of the elevator—Joe called it Marlow. Whoever got off was stopping to have a terrible coughing fit.

Joe welcomed his old friend with a hug. "How funny," she said, "To step out of Fifty-seventh Street into Dickens's London."

"This used to be a dressmakers' salon," Joe said. "I picked up the lease from the two old sisters who'd been here for decades. We're going to do it over, smarten up, get ourselves ready to be blown to kingdom come."

"Oh, leave it alone. It's dear. Have you been up to the office of Maurie's *Magazine*? The couch smells of mold. When Maurie put in the new computers he didn't remove the old wiring. It sticks out of a hole in the floor like a family of headless snakes."

"How *is* old Maurie?"

"I sent old Maurie a story called 'Rumpelstiltskin in Emergency,' which is and isn't about Bertie's last ambulance ride to the ER. I sent it to him in October! This is July." Like the Dorothy Parker heroine who spends her days and nights not calling the lover who does not call her, Lucy was *not* calling Maurie at *The Magazine*. *Why do I have this image of my little story posting outward into the ever-expanding universe?* is what she would have written if she had been going to write him. *How long can it take you to read a short-short all of three pages!*

Joe said, "I've put you in the big room with the kids. Benedict will show you around."

My poor Benedict, thought Lucy. Bethy's glare, she knew, signified hello, and she responded pleasantly. The two young men were sweet. Al Lesser spent the morning setting up Lucy's PC while Benedict showed his mother around the office. Lucy kept her eye averted from the half-eaten apple trapped among the wires that snaked out the back of Benedict's computer, and refrained from shutting the files he always left half open, until she thought he wasn't looking.

Benedict refrained from telling his mother to stop coughing.

They all took Lucy to the luncheonette downstairs. Back in the office, Joe put a batch of books on the sewing machine and said, "You might start with these."

"Will do," said Lucy, but first she checked her home answering machine. There was nothing from *The Magazine*, and Lucy took pen and paper and wrote,

> *Dear Maurie, When you and I were starting out in the Fifties, a story had a value if only in hours of typing or dollars paid the typist, and if you were not going to publish, you put the manuscript into the self-addressed and stamped envelope with a rejection slip—the time and ingenuity we wasted decoding it for degrees of encouragement! Today you're not going to return pages that printed themselves out while their author was in the kitchen making herself a sandwich, but how does that relieve you from responding with a "yes," or a "no," or the acknowledgment, merely, of receipt? How are you? How is Ulla? How old is . . .*

"Benedict, did Shari have a little boy or girl?"

"Search me."

> *... Shari's little one? Can you imagine Benedict and me working as colleagues in the same office! Did you know that Joe Bernstine has opened an office on 57th Street working on* The Compendium of End-of-World Theories, *where you can reach me during the day?*

Lucy added the office address and phone number but did not send the letter. Lucy found her glasses, picked up *Longing for the End: A History of Millennialism in Western Civilization*, by Frederic J. Baumgartner, and started reading.

When she got home that night, there was nothing from Maurie in the mail, nothing on her answering machine. There was nothing all that week, nor the next.

On the sewing machine there were always more books. Lucy proposed to stay in after Joe left for lunch and Bethy announced that she had shopping she wanted to do. Lucy observed her observing Benedict and Al refraining from exchanging looks of relief. They could go have lunch by themselves.

Lucy liked having the office to herself, and after checking that there was nothing from Maurie on her home answering machine, she settled in with a sandwich and Elaine Pagels. Came the moment when she looked up from *Visions, Prophecy, and Politics in the Book of Revelation* to search out the moldering apple, on the decomposition of which Lucy had been keeping an interested eye. Now she rose, went and dislodged the wrinkled, blackened thing from its wire nest, and threw it in the wastebasket. Energized by action, Lucy was approaching the window to remove the parade of 7UP empties from the sill, when the body fell past outside. Lucy thought, I could not have seen that body falling past the window because if I had, I would have to do something and I wouldn't know what. Stepping to the window, Lucy looked down the eleven-story shaft into the narrow gray courtyard. She saw the row of cans, the stack of bumpy, jagged black plastic garbage bags, a pot with a dead ficus, and the body, on its side, the cheek resting on the arm as if in sleep except that the left leg was bent at an angle that legs don't bend at. Now Lucy dialed 911 and reported the body of a woman, an old woman, it was a black woman, in the courtyard, and, when requested, gave her address, the number from which she was phoning, and her name.

Lucy stood at the window and watched nothing happen. In the office building across the courtyard—the building that must front 58th Street—someone sat at a computer. On the floor right above, a woman brought a plant to the window and watered it and did not know what lay in the courtyard twelve floors below, where a door had opened. A man in shirtsleeves stepped out and stood. A small wind tugged at the dead woman's skirt that was hitched up her leg in a way, Lucy thought, she would not have wanted. Lucy identified tears that constricted her throat. The man, perhaps because, like Lucy, he couldn't think of anything to do, stepped back inside and closed the door.

Al and Benedict got back from lunch and looked out the

window. Bethy and Joe returned and Joe called the building's administration. The Wide-Open Eye people tried to go back to work.

When Lucy returned to the window, the courtyard was crowded. The shirtsleeved man was there, and the police. People blocked the dead body from her view. In the building across the courtyard there were faces at the windows. The plant waterer had the view to herself, but in the window on her left, the people in the back row had to crane their necks to look over and between the heads of the people in the front.

"Interesting," Lucy said to Bethy who stood beside her, "the long beat between something happening and the world taking any notice."

"What do you mean, 'beat'?" Bethy said.

Lucy, excited and upset, was glad when Joe invited her to come home with him. At dinner Joe and Lucy told Jenny about the suicide. The beat that Lucy had noted between event and reaction interested nobody beside herself, and when she reported her own initial denial of what she had seen because she couldn't think what to do, Joe said, "All you had to do was call 911."

"Oh, I know that," said Lucy. "I did that. I just thought it was an interesting reaction, I mean, if one were writing a story. In what order would the protagonist take in what she is seeing? Is it "an old woman, unusually small, and black," or "small, black, and old," or "black, and old, and unusually small?" While she was talking Lucy observed Jenny listening with all her heart. *Her* tears were not stuck in her throat but flowed out of her eyes. *She* was not developing the dead old black woman into a story. Lucy loved her friend Jenny. Lucy said:

"I once wrote a suicide story: A woman watches a truck bearing down toward the place on the sidewalk where she stands waiting to cross. She thinks, 'If that truck were to run me over I wouldn't have to think what to get for supper.' The truck passes. The woman crosses to the supermarket and takes out her shopping list. It was called 'Truck.' Maurie published it in *The Magazine*. In the days when Maurie answered my letters."

Jenny

Breakfast was the stage on which Bethy Bernstine vented her dissatisfactions. Bethy was dissatisfied with her father, with his Wide-Open Eye, with the country, the world. "Do we ask ourselves what we have done to that African American woman to make her jump out of her own skin?"

"Yes," said her father. "We ask ourselves."

"And what do we tell ourselves?"

"I've been thinking ..." Jenny hesitated. Was this a good or was it the worst moment to say, "There are also things we do that are nice ..."

"You mean like making unnecessary wars?" suggested Bethy.

"I mean the small, funny things. I walked past the building site on the next block, and they're making square holes in the wooden fence so people passing on the sidewalk can watch the work in progress."

Bethy had perfected the stare of exaggerated disbelief: " 'Happy Days' in the sandbox, Winnie."

"And the doggie bag," persisted Jenny. "That's friendly, sensible, and I think it's an entirely American invention."

"Mom, Jesus! We're the state terrorists in the people-killing business."

"We are that too!" agreed her mother eagerly.

"How," Jenny asked Joe, after Bethy banged out of the room, "is she making out in the office?"

"She's not 'making out' with Benedict or Al, if that's what you're waiting for. That's not going to happen."

"What do you mean? I'm not waiting for anything. Don't be silly," said Jenny. "Benedict lives with that nice Viennese girl. Al Lesser is too young for her."

Jenny came to the door to see her husband and daughter off. "I've got an appointment with Dr. Switt this morning. He's two blocks from your office. Why don't I take the two of you out to lunch?"

"Sounds good," said Joe.

"Thanks, but no thanks," said Bethy.

Jenny went down the elevator with Mrs. Pontefiore. The weather lasted them the eight floors to the lobby, but conversation all the way to the corner was going to be a chore. At the front door Jenny Bernstine and Mrs. Pontefiore parted with a mutual fiction of going in opposite directions. However,

Jenny accelerated her step so as to fall in with a newer neighbor. She didn't know the name of the young woman whose short black hair bobbed along beside her. They had got the weather out of the way by agreeing they loved the midsummer city, when Jenny's companion let out a laugh.

"What?"

The young neighbor laughed again but shook her head. Jenny wouldn't let it pass.

"Nothing. That baby in the stroller smiling at its mother and the mother smiling. I mean, nothing."

Jenny said, "Yesterday, I was annoyed with my cabbie for not getting a move on. *He* was smiling at the cab that was stopped in front of us with its door open. My cabbie said, 'The kid's left his bear on the back seat.' I tell my daughter—New York is a turn-on!"

"Oh, oh, it is!" the young neighbor agreed.

"My husband believes the terrorists are going to blow us up."

"Probably are," said the young neighbor and, opening her handbag, found a quarter which she dropped without breaking stride into the parking meter so that the meter maid aborted the ticket she had begun to write. And Jenny Bernstine had her subject for conversation: "You don't find it tiresome to own a car in Manhattan?"

"Wouldn't dream of it."

"Whose car did you just save from getting a ticket?"

"Oh ..." The young woman turned to look briefly in both directions, said, "I don't really know," and raising her hand in a good-bye, started down the subway steps.

Jenny had come to confess to Dr. Switt: She was not taking her anti-depression pills. "It's that I don't *feel* depressed." Jenny told the doctor about the baby and the mother smiling at each other; about the cabbie and the teddy bear, and about the neighbor who saved a fellow citizen she didn't know from being ticketed.

The doctor on the other side of the desk had the awkward air of a man not getting a joke. He said, "It takes time to combine the right medications in the right dosage."

Joe was not going out. Jenny's arrival coincided with a delivery of books and Joe thought he would stay in and get sorted.

"Bethy and I will have lunch. What's a good place around here?"

Bethy said, "Mom. I told you this morning, No! N. O."

Lucy said, "*I'm* taking Jenny to lunch in my new favorite restaurant—just two blocks."

Lucy and Jenny

The two friends passed an interesting older couple seated by the window. "They got my table!" Lucy complained to the unsmiling proprietress of the Café Provence. "But here will be fine if you bring us some of your good bread."

Lucy and Jenny sat and ate the good bread. Lucy kept looking with a widow's eye at the man and woman at the window table. "They look as if they're in the habit of conversation," she said.

"So are you and I," Jenny said. "My neighbor and I ride down the elevator that *feels* like such a neat little cabinet made for intimacy, but Mrs. Pontefiore and I talk about the weather. Mrs. Pontefiore and I don't know, and don't care to know, anything about each other's lives. Why don't we? You and I have been talking for more than half a century and we're still talking."

What did these two old friends talk *about*? Their conversation had two trajectories. One was circular, always looping backward over familiar matters; while the loops looped incrementally in the other, bringing them from their graduation holiday in Venice with Joe and Bertie, the two men whom they might or might not have been going to marry, to this lunch at the Café Provence on 57th Street.

Lucy told Jenny about Maurie neither accepting nor rejecting her story called "Rumpelstiltskin in Emergency," which she had sent to *The Magazine* in October, she said. "This is July! How long can it take someone to read a three-page short-short?" Lucy always wondered but never asked Jenny if *Jenny* read her stories.

And they talked about the children. Jenny said, "My poor Bethy! Is she too unhappy, too cross, or maybe just too mean to just let me take her out to lunch?"

Lucy said, "I remember watching my little Benedict on his way to the bathroom. I'd say, 'You need a haircut.' I'd watch him coming out of the bathroom and I'd say, 'Tuck in your shirt!' You look at them with your chest in a riot of love wanting them to *be* happy, to *tuck* in their shirt. Today, in the office, *I* knew that picking up a grown son's sweats from underneath his chair impinges on his liberty, so I did it quick, quick, like gulping forbidden food before the calories have time to register."

Jenny was thinking about Bethy. "She says I don't talk about the real—the front-page matters, and, Lucy, I was thinking, the day you came to my place and we had lunch—do you remember if we even mentioned the tsunami? Did we used to talk about the Berlin Crisis? The Rosenbergs? McCarthy, Sputnik, the Cuban missiles, the Six-Day War? Watergate? Yes. The Kennedy assassination—everybody talked. Selma? Vietnam ..."

"Our dinner parties!" remembered Lucy.

"MoMA was our midtown club. The theater was mostly beyond our means. The Opera was never our thing."

"Bertie knew where to find the good jazz. And then you and Joe were in Connecticut, running Concordance. Bertie is dead. And you're back, and we are two old women, and we're talking."

An ambulance passed outside. Lucy said, "I get this familiar taste of gall—but, curiously, in my gut." She located the proprietress, who was talking with the couple by the window, caught her eye and signed a check in the air.

"Come with me," Jenny said. "Now I'm downtown, I want to go window shopping."

"Can't!" said Lucy. "I have to get back to the office and read Mary Shelley's *The Last Man*."

Jack and Hope

The couple who had gotten Lucy's favorite table were Jack and Hope. Jack had phoned Hope, suggested lunch, and said, "I have an agenda." No need to specify the Café Provence or the time, fifteen minutes before noon, when they were sure of getting their table by the window. The proprietress brought the menu and told them the specials. Hope said, "I always mean to order something different," but ordered the onion soup. Jack ordered the cassoulet saying, "I should have fish."

"And a bottle of your Merlot," he told the proprietress, "which we will have right away."

"We'll share a salad," said Hope. She saw Jack watch the proprietress walk away in the direction of the bar in a remarkably short skirt for a woman in her fifties. Hope watched the long, brown, athletic legs with Jack's eyes. She looked at Jack, a large man with a large dark bearded face. He turned to Hope.

"So?"

"Okay, I guess. You?"

Jack said, "My agenda: If it were New Year's and we were making resolutions, what would yours be?"

Hope's interest pricked right up. "I'm thinking. You go first."

Jack said, "Jeremy tells me I've got to watch what I eat." Jeremy was Jack's son. "Idea for a *New Yorker* cartoon: Fat man eating a whole capon in front of a mirror. Legend 'Henry the Eighth watches what he eats.' "

Hope said, "To watch what I watch and then turn the TV off. It feels debauched waking in the morning with the thing flickering."

Jack said, "No more buying books from Amazon till I've read the ones on my shelves."

Hope said, "Hanging my clothes in the closet even if nobody is coming over. Nora is very severe with me." Nora was Hope's daughter.

The wine arrived. Jack did his label checking, cork sniffing, tasting. He nodded. The salad came. Hope served their two plates. "In Provence it came after the main course."

Jack indicated Hope's hair, which she had done in an upsweep.

"Very fetching," he commented.

"Thank you. And my old resolution: What was her name—my French teacher after we got back from Paris. I once counted nine years of school French—and you had to do all the talking."

Jack said, "To learn how to pray."

Hope looked across the table to see if he was being funny. Jack concentrated on folding a whole lettuce leaf into his mouth.

Hope said, "I will never understand the principle of not cutting it into bite sizes."

The onion soup came; the cassoulet came. Jack asked Hope if she would like to go back.

"Back! Go back to Provence?"

"To Aix, to Paris."

Jack and Hope had lived together, before marrying two

other people. Jack subsequently divorced his wife who had subsequently died. Hope was widowed.

"There's something I've been thinking of asking you," Hope said. "Were you and I ever together in a very old garden? Do you remember walking under century-old trees? Where was it we lay in the grass and looked into the crown of a tree? France? Was it in England? Or is this a garden in a book?"

"What's to stop us going back?" Jack said.

There were reasons, of course, that stopped them. Two of the littlest were this moment flattening their noses against the outside of the restaurant window.

Eight-year-old John stuck his thumbs in his ears and wiggled his fingers at his grandfather. Hope made as if to catch her granddaughter's hands through the glass. Little Miranda laughed. On the sidewalk stood Hope's daughter, Nora, with baby Julia in the stroller. She had come to fetch her mother. Jack's son, Jeremy, had come to get his father.

"I'm just going to the bathroom," Hope mouthed to her daughter through the glass.

"*What?*" Nora mouthed back, her elegant features sharpened with irritation. The baby was howling and a wailing ambulance passed at her back. "She has to *know* I can't hear her," Nora said to Jeremy.

Jeremy told Nora to stay with the kids. "I'll go in and get him and see what she wants."

In the doorway, Jeremy stepped back to let Jenny and

Lucy come out. He walked straight to the corner where, an hour earlier, he had folded up his father's wheelchair and wheeled it to the table.

Hope stood up. She came around to kiss Jack and be kissed good-bye.

"On the double, Dad!" said Jeremy. "I need to get back to the office."

"I'll phone you," Jack said to Hope, "and we'll have lunch."

Hope was mouthing to Nora again.

"Julie, shut up, *please*!" Nora said, and the baby started screeching. "*WHAT*, Mom!"

Hope stabbed a finger in the direction of the ladies' room.

Nora signaled, "You need *me*," pointing at herself, "to go with *you*?" pointing at Hope. Hope shook her head no. One of the reasons for the Café Provence was that its bathrooms were on the street floor, not in the basement down a long stair.

Hope opened the door into the ladies' room and saw, in the mirror above the basins, how her hair was coming out of its pins. She removed all the pins and stood gazing at the crone with the gray, girlishly loosened locks around her shoulders and saw what Diane Arbus might have seen and was appalled, and being appalled pricked her interest right up: "I've got an agenda: The Arbus Factor of old age," Hope looked forward to saying to Jack the next time it would be convenient for Jeremy and Nora to arrange lunch for them at the Café Provence.

Jenny

Summer, and Manhattan lies tranced, lush, and melancholy with the absence of friends traveling abroad, or away in their houses by summer ponds, or a hop and a skip from the ocean beaches. The afternoon belongs all to Jenny. Not a person in the world—well, Lucy—knows that she is walking on "the Fifth Avenue," as Henry James called it, a tourist in her own city. Jenny is surprised all over again at the gigantism of the new glass structures. When did this block and the next turn seedy and brutal? Jenny follows the old glamour on its move a block to the east. Here, behind the great plate glass, is a single, delicious, appalling, little, translucent, winged, thousand-dollar cotton blouse.

Jenny walks and keeps walking, passing store after store before she gets herself to enter one through its high glass double doors. The interior was designed by Gehry.

Is it the subliminal retreat of Jenny Bernstine's head downward between her shoulders that cues the expression peculiar to ruminating camels and unoccupied salesladies in Madison Avenue boutiques? The saleslady intuits the approach—sees hovering on the outskirts of her domain, the type of wrong—the non-customer.

Jenny smiles into the Madison Avenue boutique saleslady's grossly inhospitable eyes. "I used to dream," she tells her, "when I was a girl, of such a dress. A gown!" Jenny lets the tea-colored liquefaction glide across the back of her hand. "I'd *love* to get my daughter a tea-colored gown! It's that grown-up daughters wouldn't be caught dead in a ditch wearing something their mom has picked out for them," chattered Jenny. "What I could do is buy it for myself, and then my daughter can come and borrow it?"

Has the Madison Avenue saleslady missed her cue? Her facial expression undergoes an alteration. There was a game with which Joe used to amuse little Bethy. He would arrange his face into the tragic mask and wipe it away with an upward sweep of his open hand, revealing his comic grin. The saleslady's smirk registers her readiness to be of service to the customer who might turn out to be a live one: If the young lady has brunette coloring, these golden notes would be a perfect accent.

"She's a reddish blonde, like San Giuliano."

Beautiful, and which this color, believes the saleslady, would particularly complement.

"I think you're right," agrees the customer, "except that tea-colored silk would radically disagree with my daughter's politics."

The smile goes out and reveals the look, on the Madison Avenue saleslady's face, of a terminal discouragement. She's no youngster; her salary makes for a sorry living without commissions from the sales to the customers traveling abroad or away in their houses by summer ponds, or near the ocean beaches. Her look of defeat accompanies Jenny on the escalator to the upscale floors. It hangs like an odor about the collections with designer names known to those in the know about the human genius that expresses itself in winged cotton blouses partnered with nine-inch see-through skirts and coats of many colors that it wouldn't occur to you and me to put next to each other—embroidered cloths / Enwrought with golden and silver light / The blue and the dim and the dark, and the speckled, stippled, freckled, dappled stuffs which—the sales lady was right the first time—Jenny is not going to buy, and Bethy will never wear the tea-colored gown to Cinderella's ball.

Bethy

Bethy had tried to reach her mother, but nobody knew where Lucy had taken Jenny to lunch. Neither of them had a cell phone, so it was not till she got home, in the late afternoon, that Jenny learned Joe had stopped breathing and the ambulance had taken him to Emergency at Cedars of Lebanon.

By the time Jenny, her face wizened and diminished by terror, forged through the curtains of his cubicle, Joe was grinning at her from his gurney, and Bethy, having survived her own hell of fright, was letting him have it.

"He knew something was wrong at lunchtime when you came up to the office," she shouted, "but he went right ahead unpacking his apocalypses!"

Joe said, "You tell yourself, 'If I am doing what I do when I'm all right, I must be all right.' "

"What are you smiling *about*?" screamed Bethy, beside herself.

"Bethy!" said Jenny.

"Not being dead yet," Joe said.

"You know what Al calls you behind your back? Smiley-face!"

"Beth. Please!"

"Benedict says it's your antique grin in the bone."

"That's rather good," her father said.

The young and pretty Dr. Miriam Haddad walked in. She had Joe Bernstine's record and said, "Your vitals are good, but Dr. Stimson, our head of Emergency, would like to keep you in Observation over the weekend. Just to see what is going on."

"Darling," Jenny says to Bethy the next day, "There's no need really for you to sit around here."

"If there's no need, really, why are you sitting around?" Bethy says. "If you are sitting, why wouldn't I sit?"

So they both sit with Joe.

"Why is he even lying in bed?" says Bethy. "He's not *that* sick." Bethy gets up, walks to the TV, and puts it on. Joe turns on his side to watch the vintage movie. The hero's evening dress shows that he has a waist. He has shoulders and a flat stomach. This is the hero, in evening dress, who climbs out of a window.

Joe says, "Turn it off."

Bethy says, "Why?"

The man in evening dress has stood up so that the points of his evening shoes jut over the narrow ledge.

"Turn it off," says Joe.

Jenny says, "Bethy, please, turn the TV off."

"I'm not turning it off."

Joe has turned his face to the wall but looks around to check on the man on the ledge, who has spread his hands seeking contact with the wall behind him and inches himself along the ledge looking down at the pygmy traffic on the move so many stories below. Joe sits up, struggling to untangle his legs from the sheet to find the ground under his feet.

"Where are you going?" Bethy asks her father.

"The bathroom."

"Bethy!" pleads Jenny.

"*What* is his *problem*?"

"He's not well."

"He is too, well. The doctor says his vitals are good!"

Jenny and Bethy watch the movie. They hear Joe moving around inside the little bathroom.

"Dad! You can come out! He's found a window and is climbing back in!"

"Bethy, don't."

"Bethy don't *what*?"

Joe comes out of the bathroom and gets into bed. They watch the movie. In the room the man in evening dress has climbed into stands a desk. The man in evening dress opens the right top drawer, lifts out a first item, drops it back, lifts out a second item. No audience would sit still for the real time a real search would take, so he opens the lower drawer. His back is to the door through which the man with the gun may at any moment enter.

"Turn it off," begs Joe. "Please."

"What is your problem!" shouts Bethy.

Jenny rises and turns the TV off and says, "Darling, go find me a cup of coffee."

"The Wide-Open Eye that can't watch a stupid guy on a ledge in a stupid movie!" screams Bethy.

"Bethy. Please, now."

"The Definitive Apocalypse Collector!" Bethy tosses back from the doorway.

On the way home, Bethy suffered her mother's hand to cover her fist. In the bliss of her reprieve, Jenny yearned toward her child. The intuition that Bethy would refuse to be amused by smiling mothers and their babies and taxi drivers with imaginative hearts made Jenny herself doubt their important little charms so that she told her story badly. "You know the new neighbor on the sixth floor," she asked Bethy, "who moved in a month ago?"

"So?" Bethy said.

"She put a quarter in the meter to stop somebody's car from getting ticketed—a person she didn't even know."

Bethy stared at her mother as if she were an alien from a developing planet.

Jenny thought, She is an unpleasant woman, my poor darling, and wondered how long it would take her to forget having thought this.

Lilly and Sadie

Jenny had brought Joe his own bathrobe, and he was wandering around the Observation Area when he thought he recognized the old, queen-size black woman with the arthritis-deformed hands. She was the elder of the two sisters whose defunct sewing business had been converted into the Wide-Open Eye offices. Lilly Cobbler in a wheelchair? Joe went over to claim acquaintance, but the old woman was asleep with her mouth hanging open as if it were unhinged, and Joe kept walking. He returned once, and again, and when he saw that her eyes were open, he went over and said, "It's Mrs. Cobbler, isn't it? Joe Bernstine from Fifty-seventh Street. What are you and I doing here!"

Lilly Cobbler's face suffered no alteration; the eyes evinced none of the signs of recognition nor, for that matter, of sight. The tongue worked restlessly inside the open mouth.

One day, when he was a boy, Joe had spotted a tabby cat slinking along the base of a hedge of privet. The hand he put out to pet the silken fur had encountered rigor mortis. The child leapt backward from the animal's body vacated by life with the same horror with which the man backed off from Lilly Cobbler's body vacated by mind. He turned and Dr. Haddad was walking toward him. "What's happened to Lilly Cobbler?"

"You know her?"

"Yes. What's the matter with her?"

"And did you happen to know her sister?"

"Sadie Woodway, the younger one, yes." Joe gave a brief account of his business dealings with the two dressmakers. "It was Sadie who attended the closing with the lawyer. Afterward, she and I went down and had some coffee and talked."

Dr. Haddad asked Joe if he would mind talking to her husband, Salman. Salman Haddad was Cedars of Lebanon's chief security officer. Dr. Haddad called his office, but he was out. Nor could she reach Dr. Stimson, who had added the sisters to his log of disturbed sixty-two-pluses—one catatonic and the other who had turned out to be suicidal. Dr. Haddad asked Joe Bernstine if he knew that Sadie Woodway had killed herself.

"Sadie! No way. Sadie Woodway?"

"Jumped off the roof on Fifty-seventh Street."

"That was our Sadie?" Joe was struggling to superimpose the body in the courtyard onto the woman who had sat across the table from him holding her cup not by its handle but wrapped in her two hands. His chest, where he understood his heart to be, contracted. Here Lucy Friedgold arrived to visit Joe. He introduced her to the doctor as the member of his staff who had actually witnessed the suicide. He told Lucy, "Turns out she was one of the two dressmakers whose rooms we took over! Sadie Woodway had a nice laugh," Joe told Dr. Haddad. "She thought it was hilarious that she turned out to have this flair for designing ugly men's shirts for the U.S. Open—shirts with multilayered appliqués and—what do I know?—two-colored armpit insets. Next year they would tell her, 'Make it the same but different.'

Sadie had this little internal laugh as if she'd swallowed a giggle and was afraid she wouldn't be able to stop. What," Joe looked around, distraught, "is the chance of getting a cup of coffee?"

"Me too," Dr. Haddad said. "You?" she asked Lucy. She beckoned over one of the nurse's aides.

Joe said, "I think it was rough on both of them giving up the business, but Lilly's hands were becoming too painful for her to work, and Sadie was having trouble with her heart."

"That's why her sister brought her to the ER," Dr. Haddad said.

"How old was Sadie?" asked Lucy.

"Old enough," remembered Joe, "to complain of forgetting the names of customers she'd known for years. They had a hand signal meaning, 'Call this customer by her name because I can't remember which one she is.' I said—you know what one always says—'It happens to all of us.' Sadie said there were two customers she could never tell apart, and I remembered Nabokov's Pnin, who never taught a class that didn't have one pair of identical twins. Sadie *loved* that! 'Excuse me,' she should have said to her customer, 'but are you the twin we're letting out your old navy serge skirt for, or are you the twin come for a fitting of the mauve silk mother-of-the-bride costume?' And she'd do her internal giggle. I can't—I just don't see Sadie Woodway jumping out of the window."

Dr. Haddad said, "The roof."

"And Lilly Cobbler? What *happened* to her?"

"They presented like two sensible women—the big one,

Lilly, reasonably anxious when she brought her sister into the ER. Sadie was having palpitations. This was a Saturday. We gave her a referral to come back Monday to see the cardiologist, but Sunday morning, Sadie, the little one, brings in Lilly the way you see her now. Stays with her that whole day. Nurse alerts me to come and take a look. The two of us watch. Sadie is holding Lilly's mouth to make it stay closed."

The aide arrived with their coffee in three paper cups standing upright in three holes in a cardboard tray.

"I brought cookies. We have a picnic," said Lucy sadly.

"Sadie spoons a little water into Lilly's mouth," went on Dr. Haddad, "and Lilly's tongue pushes the water out. So then Sadie passes this little bottle of perfume under Lilly's nose and goes 'Sniff sniff sniff, Lilly! Lilly, smell this!' Lilly sits with her mouth open. Sadie strokes her sister's right temple, her left temple, both temples, chafes her cheek, pats it with a little slap, chafes, slaps, and chafes. She finds her sister's foot under the sheet and massages it.

"When I went in Sadie was holding a photograph in front of her sister's eyes. I asked if I might see: Big African American picnic. Little children sitting cross-legged on the grass and on the laps of the women on chairs in the first row, second row standing, rows and rows, everybody in a good mood. Sadie said at last count there were seventy-four Woodways. The great granddad brought his family north to Seattle. Now, of course, she said, everybody lives all over. Lilly's husband died—he was from Chicago—Sadie, never married. Anyway, they came to New York and started sewing and did all right. Said that everybody goes to Seattle every five years for the family barbecue. Sadie said she'd stick close to her sister, who was fourteen when they left. Sadie was maybe nine? Lilly remembered the names of all the aunts and which cousin was married to whom and who had passed on, and if she didn't remember the names of their children, she just went ahead and asked.

"The police have been here twice: The building super saw Sadie Woodway enter the elevator around eight in the morning—said he had known her and her sister for twenty years and thought nothing of it. She must have taken the elevator to the roof, but didn't jump till noon. The police have been talking to my husband."

It was here that Joe suggested how he and his staff might be helpful in relation to what, he thought, might be afoot in the Cedars of Lebanon's ER. "If you're interested," he said to Dr. Haddad, "you might want to Google me. Check out my work at the Concordance Center."

Dr. Miriam Haddad

But before Dr. Haddad Googled Joe Bernstine, she called the hospital's legal department and told them that she had disclosed two patients' health information to a third party.

Was the third party a family member or involved in the patients' care, the legal department asked her. They were not? No problem. If the doctor would look at a copy of the Cedars of Lebanon's Notice of Privacy Practices (which all patients were required to sign, though no one had ever been known to actually read it) all Dr. Haddad needed to do was have the patients sign "an authorization for the sharing of their health information."

One of the two patients was catatonic and the other dead? In that case, offered the legal department, these were not patients likely to exercise their right "to receive an accounting of such disclosures." And there were in any case the three exceptions that permitted patient information to be disclosed to a third party, if the doctor would look at— Here the legal department took a moment to count down to line 32: Exception [1] "To facilitate treatment," [2] "To collect payment," and [3] "General hospital business," where the latter can usually be understood to cover all remaining contingencies. If there was anything, the legal department said, in which the legal department could be of further assistance, Dr. Haddad was not to hesitate to call.

Dr. Miriam Haddad and Salman Haddad Googled Joseph Bernstine's twenty-year association with the respected Concordance Center, of which he had been a co-founder and, for eleven years, director. The Center's Washington ties and its list of consultants, including two Nobel laureates, were impressive.

"We're meeting Dad at Cedars of Lebanon," Bethy informed Benedict when he arrived at the office.

"I thought he was getting out this morning."

"*Is* out. Our regular Monday meeting, only at Cedars."

"Where's my mom?"

"How would *I* know?" offered Bethy.

"I mean is *she* at Cedars. Isn't sick, is she?"

"Search me. Dad says to get her a cell phone."

"A cell for my mom? She doesn't know how to use a cell."

"Dad says to show her."

"This is where my dad died," Benedict said. He followed Al and Bethy through the revolving doors. They tipped back their heads to look up into the atrium's high vaulted ceiling.

"A young cathedral," Al said.

"Giant fucking air container," Benedict said.

They thought they were alone with the janitor, who was circling an industrial floor polisher around and around the expanse of blond marble, when Joe Bernstine said, "Hello there!" He hopped off the ledge of a marble basin where golden fish swam around an island from which grew a twenty-foot-high stand of bamboo. Another stand grew from another such basin over by the east entrance. Behind its great glass doors Benedict was relieved to make out his mother queuing at a Starbucks wagon.

"Getting us lattes," Joe said.

Benedict scrunched up his eyes. "She doesn't look sick or anything."

Joe silenced him with a motion of the head that appeared to refer Benedict to the giant grasses and mouthed: "Might be bugged."

"Joe and his bugs," Benedict said aside to Al, who laughed. Both assumed, mistakenly, that Joe's account of a nifty piece of technology he called a "reverse bug," which could be introduced into a room to broadcast to those on the inside the information they would have chosen not to hear, was another of his funny ideas. They followed their little boss to the center of the vast space, where a second janitor arrived with a set of nested designer chairs that he arranged in a circle.

"Sit down," said Joe, "and keep your eyes skinned."

"For what?" asked Bethy.

What was there to look at? A nicely coiffured elderly volunteer rummaging in a large handbag found her keys and unlocked a door. After a moment, the lights came on inside the hospital's gift shop, the shelves of which specialized in objects that were not beautiful, interesting, or useful, and which nobody could be imagined to wish to own. Half a dozen interns, their white coats flapping open, with the good faces of people who have the stamina for extended study, moved briskly toward the east elevators. They were laughing.

Lucy came toward them walking on her upside-down reflection in the high polish of the floor. She carried two paper cups and she was coughing.

"We'll have no trouble getting her past triage," Joe said.

"What for?" Benedict asked, but Joe was rising from his

chair. They all got up. Joe introduced his staff to Dr. Haddad: "You've met Lucy Friedgold, you remember, who happened to see the suicide; her son, Benedict Friedgold. Al Lesser. My daughter, Beth Bernstine. Dr. Haddad is going to brief us on a situation in the ER."

"Our Chief of Emergency, Dr. Stimson, has been called away and has asked me to be the liaison. Mr. Bernstine likes calling it 'copycat Alzheimer's,' whatever it is that we're looking at. Alzheimer's, of course, develops over decades, a lifetime, generations, and we seem to be watching patients becoming demented in front of our eyes. You," Dr. Haddad said to Joe, "were in Emergency when Anstiss Adams went off the deep end. I'd always thought of her as the sanest person I know."

"What did she do?" asked Bethy.

"How old was she?" asked Lucy.

"Ninety-plus," said the doctor.

Lucy did the arithmetic. At seventy-five, Lucy was at least fifteen years younger than Anstiss, who had gone off the deep end. Lucy experienced relief.

Joe asked, "And when did you become aware of the unusual number of patients becoming demented? We're talking of the sixty-two pluses?"

"Yes," Dr. Haddad said. "Dr. Stimson began keeping his log—it happened to be the day you yourself checked in the last time around."

"And what do these patients do?" asked Bethy.

Al said, "Don't old people just naturally *get* demented?" Al had a grandmother.

"All the time, but never this many of them."

"How many is this many?"

"Well, every one of the sixty-two-pluses," said the doctor. And Bethy thought, If nobody is going to pay attention to my question, I'm not going to say another word.

Dr. Haddad said, "One came in this morning, wheelchair, the son brought him in, eighty-five-year-old male with diabetes and associated problems. He started to cry and he cries and cries and cannot seem to stop."

Eighty-five minus seventy-five: The diabetes with associated problems was ten years older than Lucy.

"And your friends, Mr. Bernstine, Lilly Cobbler and Sadie Woodway. It's the happenstance of Mr. Bernstine's acquaintance with the suicide and his input in the ongoing investigation that has suggested some sort of cooperation between your organization and the ER."

This was news to the Compendium people—it gave them a turn to think that the dead woman in the courtyard had been alive and walking in the spaces in which they walked, in which they sat at their computers.

Dr. Haddad told them how Lilly Cobbler had brought in her sister, "One of those Saturday nights from hell. What we need is an adequate ER."

"Why don't you take over the underpopulated atrium?" proposed Benedict. He had been trying to connect with the doctor's eye. She was young, had a flower face, and wore retro glasses with light-blue frames, and that interesting scarf that entirely covered her hair; its two ends hung to her waist. Her speech was crisp and quick with the hint of a lisp.

"All we were likely to do," she said, "was add god-knows-what infection on top of her heart failure, so we gave her a referral to come back on Monday to see our cardiologist, but the two sisters were the first patients in the waiting area Sunday morning—one catatonic, the other, as it turned out, suicidal."

"Sisters," suggested Benedict. "Mightn't they have the same dementia gene?"

"They might, but what's the statistical likelihood of it coming to full bloom in both in the same twelve hours?"

Lucy suggested, "Stress! Sadie was sick, Lilly was scared, and you sent them home?"

"But Sadie's vitals were normal! I sent my head nurse to check her out, and her vitals were normal! Nurse Gomez diagnosed sudden-onset white hair."

Al said, "My nana suffered sudden-onset red hair."

"But what is suddenly driving every one of our older patients around the bend?"

Benedict asked, "And where exactly do we come in?"

"Mr. Bernstine has advanced the possibility that there might be entities that have an interest in manipulating—let's call it Alzheimer's—into an epidemic."

"Joe!" cried Benedict, "An Alzheimer's epidemic! Better than the common cold!" Now, Benedict knew better than to air an office joke in public, but it irked him that the pretty doctor continued to keep her intelligent eye on Uncle Joe Bernstine.

"Ordinarily, as Mr. Bernstine says, all you would do is wonder, but now you think, what if in twelve months, we're sitting in a congressional hearing and someone asks 'How come you didn't connect the dots?'"

Benedict said, "What if they ask why you didn't report an epidemic to the Centers for Disease Control?"

"Because," Joe said, "at the moment there isn't anything *to* report. You," he said to Benedict, "will research types of dementia and the known causes of each."

"About these entities," Benedict asked Joe. "How are they understood to be manipulating what happens inside the confines of the ER?"

"That's what we are going to find out," Joe said. "Legionnaires' disease was spread through the air conditioning. Water can be contaminated. There are rats, mosquitoes; bio- and radiological hazards. There are odorless gases. The person who, some years back, tampered with pill bottles is at large. So is the sender of anthrax through the mail. Lucy, we've arranged for you to spend the night in the ER to look around."

"What am I looking around for?" Lucy was worried.

"Dots and entities," said Benedict.

Joe said, "Lucy, I remember our Venice trip. It got to be a joke, your telling us what the rest of us had been looking at and never noticed? You'll check in as a regular patient and observe what you observe."

"And I'll be on night duty," Dr. Haddad said.

Joe said, "I'll check myself in in the morning and cover the next twelve day hours. Lucy, Benedict will show you how your new cell phone works, in case we need to contact you. Benedict, Beth, Al, you'll see Dr. Haddad's husband,

Salman Haddad, in security. He will infiltrate you into the Social Service department. You'll interview the incoming sixty-two-pluses. Dr. Haddad, might there be a holding area where we could isolate the patients who have, and who may, become demented? Meanwhile, if you see Lucy in the ER, you don't know her," Joe said. "For the moment we will keep what's going on under wraps. No use alarming the hospital population till we have something to report. Rumor and speculation would be counterproductive. But I would like to set up a meeting with the the principals."

"In my husband's office on the fourth floor of the Seymour D. and Vivian L. Levi Pavilion," proposed Dr. Haddad.

Lucy said, "Just show me how to answer a cell phone. When would I ever need to make a call?"

"*Mom!*"

"Okay, so how to make and answer calls. I don't want to know about voice mails and menus and things."

The two generations had a bad time of it. Lucy could not imagine what it was that Benedict understood, and Benedict couldn't imagine anybody not understanding it. He sat beside her and pressed buttons. Lucy said, "What did you just do? I don't know what you did. Benedict, you need to let *me* do it."

"So press Code Entry."

"Which is that?"

"Mom! Where it says 'Code Entry.' Press."

"Press where? I don't see where it says 'Press.' "

" 'Select.' *Mom!* SELECT. Press it!"

"Oh! I see! I've pressed 'Select.' Now it says 'Code Entry' again. Should I press it?"

"MOM!"

"I *think* I got it," said Lucy after a while. "Benedict, go home. No need for you to hang around all night."

"Okay, Mom. After I see Haddad's husband. We have to go to his office and get ourselves tricked out like social workers. Mom will you be okay?"

"I'm fine."

Salman Haddad, the hospital's chief security officer, was a good ten or more years older than his wife. He was an elegant little brown man with a scholarly look, or was it the rimless glasses? His assistant was a large unsmiling woman groomed in some formal, corseted fashion. She was probably overqualified for her job and did not think it ought to be her business to be obliged to explain to yet another lot of interns that it was Phyllis on the second floor they needed to talk to.

Phyllis on the second floor was a cheerful, plump, competent woman who looked at home on her chair behind her desk. She set Bethy, Benedict, and Al Lesser up with identification tags, clipboards, and batches of Intake Forms for Seniors. Mostly they'd be seeing patients in the ER or on the floors, but Phyllis walked them down the corridor and unlocked the door to a windowless cubby.

Benedict said, "Bigger than a breadbox, smaller than a broom closet."

"Used to *be* a broom closet," said Phyllis. "Two desks, two chairs, and a chair for the patient. You," she said to Bethy, "can use one of the desks in my office." Bethy, instead of thinking Sexism!, thought, Because it's me, and her heart was sore and angry to have been assigned no desk in the broom closet, and with a free-floating soreness reinforced by the intuition that her father and mother's hearts were sore for her.

"You'll do Rhinelander, Francis," Phyllis said to Al. "Blacked out in his hotel."

"What if I don't know the medical terms?" Al asked her.

"Don't have to. *They* take the medical histories, you do their lives. You ask them do they know where they are, and then you go down the questions on the Intake Form, write the answers on the appropriate line, bring the form back to us, and we file it."

To Benedict, she said, "Your first is Gorewitz, Samson, on his way over from Glenshore General Hospital. Cerebral accident. Possible sunstroke. Possible hypothermia."

And Bethy thought, What about me!

II
The ER

The waiting area was a familiar third world where Lucy, or Lucy and Benedict, had sat with Bertie. There was nothing for the dozen or so patients to do but sit and wait, reread the Out of Order notice attached to the candy machine, and wish they were next. Today, of course, Lucy was here as an observer. How could she have left home without a book!

The door opened and here came two new people to look at, a woman in a blue buttoned blouse who was leading a crooked old body by the elbow. The old person looked all nose and chin; the woman in the blouse, neither old nor fat, had abandoned the search for a shape. Her bare legs were mapped with varicose veins. She led the old person to the bench next to Lucy and said, "Sit. You sit here, okay?" and then she went and waited behind an unusually tall old man with a smashed face, who had to bend his head to talk with the nurse through the triage window. When he had finished and gone to sit down, the woman in the blouse talked with the nurse. "She's my neighbor. Name is Ida Farkasz, except she doesn't remember. She doesn't remember which is her apartment or anything, and I got to get home, I have my own things I have to do. My name? Sophie Bauer," and Sophie Bauer mentioned that she was no spring chicken herself.

"Well, none of us are," said the triage nurse.

Ida Farkasz

Poor Sophie Bauer. The Good Samaritan, having accomplished his storied deed of compassion, returned, we suppose, to Samaria, but Sophie Bauer lived on the same staircase as old Ida Farkasz.

"It's a wonder they leave her live by herself," Sophie had made the mistake of saying to her married daughter, Sally, who was visiting from Queens, because Sally got exercised and gave her mother a hard time.

"I don't see why you have to even get involved!" Sally shouted. "What is she, Polish or what? If something happens, you want to be responsible?"

"So what do you want me, to leave her walking up and down the lobby downstairs?" Sophie had found the old woman muttering, snorting, aborting an occasional note like a howl. Sophie Bauer understood that she, Sophie, was not the object of the old woman's passion of spite; that Ida Farkasz did not recognize—wasn't conscious, perhaps—of the person of the neighbor who was walking her up the stairs to her apartment.

"You want, I'll unlock it for you," said Sophie, and Ida

Farkasz had walked in without turning around, and shut the door.

"Why don't her people take care of her!" shouted Sally.

"Marta, the daughter, visits her, and there's a sister, Poldi, but she doesn't come around anymore."

Sophie, on the floor right below, couldn't help hearing, if she just cracked her front door, when they were carrying on up there. She'd peek and she'd see Poldi coming down the stairs. Poldi was quite the opposite of Ida. The brim of Poldi's hat slanted across her left eye in the fashion, in Sophie's imagination, of *entre-guerras* Vienna. Sophie would have liked to try on Poldi's hat.

"I don't see why *you* have to be everybody's caretaker," Sally had said to her mother. "I mean, you're no spring chicken yourself. Don't you have your own things you have to do?"

Then, today, when Sophie came in from marketing, Ida Farkasz was trying to open the door of Mrs. Finley's apartment on the second floor. Sophie had called to her. "Mrs. Farkasz! Mrs. Farkasz, you're one floor up! You're Three-A, don't you remember?"

"Remember," said Ida Farkasz and went on poking her key into the keyhole it was never going to fit. Sophie needed to put her bags down and get her shoes off, so she brought the old woman into her own kitchen.

"A cup of coffee, and you'll be right as rain. You sit down now. Sit down, okay?"

Ida Farkasz seemed not to remember how one goes about sitting until Sophie pulled out the chair for her and pressed down on her shoulder. She did *not* look right. She touched her forefinger to her lip, her chin, and back to her lip while the other hand allowed the key to slip to the floor. Sophie picked up the key and put it in Mrs. Farkasz's hand but the fingers did not close around it and the key slipped to the floor. Sophie had looked into Ida Farkasz's eyes and seen raw terror. Couldn't remember how she even got her into a cab to bring her to Cedars of Lebanon's Emergency.

Sophie Bauer walked back to where old Ida sat on the bench and said, "You wait here. You'll be okay, okay? They'll take care of you. Okay?" and she went home and wasn't going to even tell Sally.

Lucy smiled at the crooked old woman who glared at her over the top of her glasses that must have been fitted when the face was better fleshed, because they were on a slide down the nose for a rendezvous with the hairy chin.

The nurse called the tall old man with the banged-up face into the little triage office. His name was Francis Rhinelander and he had reached his full height in his teens, a mild-mannered boy who smiled at people when they asked him what the weather was like up there. An early habit of ducking his head grew into a permanent little bow of politeness, or was it apology? His look was patient; his smile had a sweetness. The nurse made him sit and asked him if he knew where he was, but held up her hand because she was taking his pulse. She took his pressure and his temperature.

"They did my blood at Godford Memorial in Connecticut this morning," the old man said. "I have the number."

"We do our own tests. What brings you here?"

"I passed out in the lobby of my hotel. I didn't have any breakfast."

The triage nurse fastened a bracelet with his name around his wrist and pointed to the door into the ER.

After the enforced patience on the benches and the brown light of the waiting area, Emergency looked to be lit by klieg lights, no corners or shaded places. Bertie had said, "Abandon hope of hiding out from what's going to happen. What are they going to do to me?"

The good-looking young woman on the gurney near the door had been crying for a while, and her nose and eyes were swollen red. A nurse with Mayan or it might be Asian facial structure told Lucy to go sit down where several patients waited on two rows of chairs. Here was the unusually tall man with the bruised face. Another old man holding a bloody napkin to the side of his head asked the nurse, "How long am I going to sit here?"

The nurse said, "Till it's your turn."

Lucy took a chair. In the row behind her an obese girl vomited into a kidney-shaped pan that her obese mother held under her chin. It grossed out a teenage boy—her brother? He said, "Tell her to stop already! She's not that sick!"

"She's sick," the mother said.

Please, said Lucy to the hole in the world where god would have been a good thing to have in this situation, don't let *me* be going to throw up. Bertie, on the last day, had kept vomiting.

A world in motion—doctors in white coats with stethoscopes around their necks, nurses and nurse's aides in a perpetual exchange of place. An orderly with bare, powerfully developed upper arms trundled a gurney somebody must have just gotten, or been taken, down from. Action without plot or theme and no protagonist unless it was the crying young woman. She could have been the daughter of one of Lucy's women friends. Might she be wanting somebody to talk to, or would she prefer to be left alone? What, in any case, was there to be said? Time, dear … a year from now, whatever it is will be this thing that happened. You're young, nice-looking, and middle-class.

Lucy searched through her bag for the book she knew was not there. She found her pen, the reading glasses in their case, but no paper, so she opened her address book to the empty Z page, and wrote,

> *Dear Maurie, If, on some rainy day, I lent you my umbrella you would feel obliged to return it. Why is it okay for you to hold a story of mine indefinitely, perhaps never to return it to me?*

There was a pearl-gray umbrella—Lucy knew who had left it behind—that she had been going to return one of these years.

How is it that you feel no obligation to respond with a "yes," a "no," or the acknowledgment, simply, of receipt?

Here's where the old man with the bloody napkin to his head said, "Screw it," and got up and went and stood behind two white coats, to wait for them to finish their conversation. Was Lucy allowed—was she maybe *supposed* to walk around to observe and hear everything? Lucy got up and could think of nothing better to do than to go and stand behind the old man with the bloody head. What if the two doctors were discussing the very thing that Lucy was supposed to find out? She leaned in to hear what the doctors were saying but they were talking after the fashion of the new realist actors who turn their faces toward each other and away from the audience, who cannot, consequently, hear the words they are speaking.

"I'm bleeding from my head!" the old man said out loud, at which both doctors turned and looked at him. One had a gorgeous head of young hair—he looked the type who worked out. He said, "If you'll sit down, someone will take care of you."

"A head wound?" the old man said. "Ain't I an emergency?"

"To you, you're an emergency," said the doctor who worked out. "To us you're the next case."

The old man cursed under his breath and went back to his chair. Lucy smiled the smile she would have given had she found herself sitting next to either of the doctors at a dinner party. "I think he's scared," she said to them.

"And everybody wants some idea of how long it's going to be."

"Everybody will just have to wait, won't they?" said the older doctor. He reminded Lucy of her accountant, who had been doing her taxes for the past quarter of a century. "Why," he said to Lucy, "don't you go and sit down?"

They don't know who I am, thought Lucy, offended. "I'm supposed to connect with Dr. Miriam Haddad," she said, but the doctors had returned to their conversation.

Lucy went and sat down, opened her handbag, and there, in the compartment dedicated to it, was the cell phone! Lucy found her reading glasses, took them out of their case, and had identified the "talk" button on the phone when a nurse, who looked like Betsy Trotwood, descended on her crying, "No phones in Emergency."

Lucy said, "I'm supposed to connect with Dr. Miriam Haddad."

"No phones!" said Nurse Trotwood.

The crying young woman lay still. The fat girl had another bout of vomiting. The brother said he was going to get a Coke, and the mother looked for coins in her purse.

"Hope the machine is working," Lucy said to the boy, who drew his head back and away from the old woman who was talking to him.

A young woman came and sat down next to Lucy. Her tired face was narrow and pointed with anxiety. She'd got her red sweater on inside out and it had not occurred to her to put it right. Her name was Maggie, and she was wanting to talk. She said, "They're figuring what to do with my mom. Last time, they moved her from the ER to the cardiac floor, to rehab. The rehab nurses thought my mom was going to transfer to the eleventh floor, for residents, but I thought I could handle it. I went to the Kastel Street Social Services office," Maggie told Lucy.

"And discovered," said Lucy, "that Kafka wrote slice-of-life fiction?"

Ilka Weiss

"I've got an appointment with a Ms. Claudia Haze at Social Services," Maggie had said to her husband, Jeff. "Will you stay with the boys and look in on my mom?"

"I have an appointment downtown," Jeff had said.

Maggie asked Jeff what time he was leaving, and Jeff asked Maggie when she expected to be back.

Maggie said, "That's anybody's guess. You'll pick the boys up?"

"If I'm back in time," Jeff said, but there is no need to pursue a discussion of the daily logistics where both parties are married to their own priorities.

The man behind the desk at Kastel Street Social Services was not sure if Ms. Haze was in. He hadn't seen her around.

Maggie said, "I have a two-thirty appointment. For my mother, Ilka Weiss."

The man picked up the office intercom. He was in his fifties and had an unhealthy pallor suggesting that his skin might feel dank to the touch. He wore a dark suit and his narrow tie looked to have been knotted by a hangman's hand. Maggie imagined a wife who had married him, who sat across from him at supper when he came home after a day behind his desk in Kastel Street, and who lay beside him in their bed. With the phone at his ear the man said, "Not at her desk. She may not be back from lunch, or have left for the day, but as I say, I haven't seen her around."

"It took me a week and a half to get this appointment!" wailed Maggie.

"What I can do," the man said, "is take down your information and leave it for her on her desk in her office."

"Oh," said Maggie, "okay. I guess. The argument I wanted to make to Ms. Haze—could I sit down?"

"Turn one of the chairs around."

"Great. Thanks. I wanted to argue the advantage to the city if the department makes it possible for me to keep my mother at home."

The man behind the desk wrote Maggie's facts on a lined yellow pad. "The visiting nurse comes Tuesdays, but we've maxed out on the four-hour, four-afternoons-a-week caregiver. She was no great shakes, but she came; she was okay."

"It's tough," the man said. His teeth were terrible but something not unsympathetic lurked about his mouth.

"Rehab had taught my mom to put her stockings and shoes on without having to bend."

"They're good," the man said. "Come a long way teaching the old people to do for themselves."

Maggie said, "I can sleep on the couch in my mom's room. When she wakes and starts putting on her stockings and her shoes, I get up and tell her, Mom, it's two o'clock, middle of the night. She shakes her head. We laugh, get her back into her bed. Twenty minutes later she's putting her stockings and her shoes on. I get up ..."

"Which you can do for one night, two nights," the man said, "but you can't *be* up night after night."

Maggie said, "So, if you could put in a request for me, for someone to sleep over every other night—say three nights a week, I think that I can manage."

"Yes, well, no, I can't do that," the man behind the desk said. "Ms. Cloudy Haze—Cloudy is what we call her in the office—is the associate in charge of night nursing. You'll need to make an appointment because she's not in her office."

"So can you make the appointment for me?"

"Well, no. Ms. Brooks is the associate that takes care of Cloudy's calendar."

Maggie said, "I eventually got a Mr. Warren on the phone, and he made the appointment for today."

"That was me," said the man behind the desk. "That was on the first of this month—which explains why your appointment didn't register—when Kastel Street was one of seven self-administrating local offices, before they reorganized us into a single citywide department under a new administrative czar whose mandate is to rid the department of the inefficiencies and inequalities that had crept into the system since the reorganization, in the Nineties, of the single citywide department, riddled with inequities and inefficiencies, into seven self-administrating local offices, but let me check for you if Ms. Brooks is at her desk in her office."

"Thank you."

The man's smile was not unpleasant. "Nope. Not in her office. If this is Ms. Brooks's field day seeing clients in their homes she wouldn't be even coming in to the office. But," the man tapped what he had written on the yellow pad, "as I said, I can put your request on Cloudy's desk for you."

"Mr. Warren, would you—Mr. Warren, please, let me take your notes and put them on Ms. Cloudy's desk myself, so I'll feel as if I've *been* here and got *something* accomplished?"

"What the heck, you go on and do it!" said the man behind the desk, who wasn't a bad sort. "Around the corner, turn left. Her name is on the door."

With Mr. Warren's notes in her hand, Maggie stood in the door of Ms. Cloudy Haze's office and took in the paper nightmare—paper stacks, towers of papers, wire baskets of in-papers and out-papers. The stapler gave Maggie the idea: From her wallet, between a snapshot of Jeff with David and a snapshot of baby Steven, Maggie took a photo of her mother and stapled it to Mr. Warren's notes and walked around to the front of Ms. Cloudy's desk. Maggie's idea was to place her mother's face where Cloudy's eyes, as she seated herself in her chair, could not help meeting Ilka's eyes, until Maggie's eyes met the eyes in all the faces stapled, glued, and paper-clipped to all the notes and letters, and correctly attached in the upper right corner of the applications waiting for Claudia Haze's perusal, determination, and appropriate action.

On her way out, Maggie went to thank Mr. Warren. He urged her in the direction of the door. "You just missed her! She's been in with a representative of the new administration. If you hurry ..."

Maggie had come out into the corridor in time to catch the tall, the towering back over-topped with hair so high and so black Maggie thought it must be a wig, of what might or might not have been Ms. Claudia Haze stepping into the elevator, which had closed its door behind her.

Lucy was glad to see Dr. Haddad walking toward her, but the doctor was coming to speak to the young woman in the inside-out red sweater. The doctor said, "You can go ahead and take your mom home." Dr. Haddad and the young woman walked away together, and Lucy saw Al Lesser hesitating in the doorway.

Al saw Lucy among the patients on the chairs and avoided her eye. He saw a fat girl asleep with her head on the shoulder of a fat mother and a teenage boy sucking on a Coke bottle. An old man who held a bloody napkin to his temple asked Al what time it was.

"I'm supposed to interview ..." Al checked the name on the Intake Form for Seniors, "Francis Rhinelander?"

The nurse had the look people must mean when they said someone had a horse face. She picked up the left arm and checked the wrist of the other old man. This one might have been a movie extra made to look as if he'd been beaten up. "Take him in the second cubicle," said Nurse Trotwood. "I'll get him a gown."

Francis Rhinelander

The old man dangled his legs over the edge of the gurney and tried in vain to pull the hem of his hospital gown down to cover his naked knees. Al asked him did he know where he was, and he did. He knew that he lived in the Hotel Strasburg on Madison Avenue. His sentences tended to end on the rising or "feminine" note as if they awaited confirmation.

Al wrote in the month, day, and a year of his birth in the second decade of the nineteen-hundreds. "Nearest relative?"

"My brother, George, in Godford, Connecticut? I just came back from a visit." The Intake Form for Seniors had no line for the brother's wife, the several nephews, or the fact that the patient had that day returned from a visit.

"Marital status?"

"I'm single." The patient did not add that he still, once in a while though never very strenuously, imagined that some pleasing, tall, and more than ordinarily forceful woman might come along and marry him.

"Education?"

"Godford High." The patient said that their house had stood on School Street so that all he, his brother, and their dad, who, he said, taught Godford Middle School math, had to do was to just cross over. "I took piano at Juilliard," said the patient.

Al said, "My mom plays the piano," and blushed, wondering whether it was okay for an interviewer to have a mom.

"And composition," Rhinelander said.

"Oh, wow." The interviewer was interested. "What did you compose?"

For a moment the old man was silent. He said, "Did you know Verdi wrote *Otello* when he was seventy-four? He was seventy-eight when he wrote *Falstaff*."

Al did not know this. "Employment history?" he asked the patient.

Until his retirement, Francis Rhinelander had taught math at Joan of Arc on Manhattan's West Side. He had never grown accustomed to the global shriek that accumulates from the individual shrieks out of young throats in confined spaces. But he had learned to suffer the small panic with which he had always opened the door to his next class. Francis Rhinelander would stand at his tall height in front of a room of leaping, circling, howling dervishes and call for order. "Will everybody come to order, please! Order! Everybody settle down! Order! Everybody!"

"Same vocabulary and same lack of effect as the speaker of our House of Commons," the humorous Brit in the next classroom said to Francis.

"And I gave private piano lessons," Rhinelander told Al.

Rhinelander mentioned that he had been responsible for producing the lower-school entertainment on annual grandparents' day. "The chorus sang 'Oh Happy Day,' the solo piano played 'Für Elise.' The first-graders had colored boomsticks and banged them together."

"That's so cute!" Al said.

"Not really. Margaret West, my Godford piano teacher, used to say you'd be surprised how many children don't have talent."

"Psychiatric history?" asked the Intake Form. Had Mr. Rhinelander ever been in therapy?

"No. Well, yes, the time I checked myself into Bellevue, after I first moved to New York."

Bellevue had transferred the patient to Upland State Hospital, where Dr. Lev Erwin was doing admissions. He asked the incoming patient what seemed to be the matter.

Rhinelander said, "I think I'm hearing music."

"Aural hallucination," the doctor penciled on his pad and said, "Hold on," got up, and walked over to the window, where he let down the venetian blinds to block the winter sun's horizontal rays. He came back, sat down, and said, "Where and when do you hear this music?"

"Think. I *think* I hear music." Having contradicted a doctor, Rhinelander smiled and ducked his head.

"When and where do you *think* you hear this music?"

"All the time, everywhere."

"Hearing the music of the spheres, are you?" joked the doctor. "What sort of music are the spheres into these days?"

"Orchestral, vocal, classical, light classical, pop, the standards, movie music, classic rock, punk, rap ..."

"Dark in here, isn't it?" The doctor got up, walked to the window, turned the plastic wand to halfway open the slats of the blinds, and came back and sat down.

The patient said, "I think I hear music in my dentist's waiting room, my hotel, in the lobby, the elevator, the cafeteria? In the *men's room*!"

"You mean Muzak," the doctor said.

"And always—I *always* hear music when there's somebody talking! This professor will be lecturing about the Cultural Revolution and I'm hearing a pentatonic *chink-chink* that I must be thinking is Chinese-type music, and so loud I have to strain to even catch the words? Particle physics and *I* think I'm hearing Philip Glass?"

"You're talking about background music," the doctor said.

"A man will be selling a car? *I think* I hear the Goldberg Variations!"

"You mean on the TV!"

"And on my little radio that I have on the chair next to my bed. This general says that making soldiers clean up after hurricanes will ruin their will to kill? I think I'm hearing Sousa."

The alternating shadow and light that striped the top of the desk, striped the patient, irritated the doctor. He got up, walked to the window, and changed the slant of the slats of the venetian blind. "Stuffy in here, isn't it?"

"A little," said the patient agreeably.

The doctor opened the window an inch at the bottom, came back, and sat down. "You tell me if it gets too cold."

"It's fine," the patient said.

"So. Let me ask you this," said the doctor. "Do you ever hear any music you *think* might really be playing—let's say on your TV?"

"Aha!" cried the patient. His ace in the hole (which he was going to repeat to his fellow inmates for the several weeks they kept him in the Upland facility): "Did you ever see that pretty girl who is brushing her teeth?"

"You mean the toothpaste commercial?"

"Right! And she smiles and brushes her teeth and sings 'Brush your teeth with Physohilo, smile the Physohilo smile, oh!'? Now," said Francis Rhinelander, "you can be brushing your teeth and be simultaneously smiling. If you think about it, you can't *be* brushing your teeth and not be smiling. And there *are* people who can simultaneously sing *and* smile, but!"

cried the patient triumphantly as if he were his own prosecutor clinching the case against himself: "You cannot—because I've tried it in front of the mirror and you cannot brush and sing and smile and I *see* her smiling and think I hear her singing 'Smile the Physohilo smile, oh!' *while* she is brushing her teeth. *Which is not possible!*"

The patient's hysterical enthusiasm made the doctor pick up the telephone. "This is Dr. Erwin in admissions. See who's on duty, will you?" The doctor, with the phone to his ear, turned to frown at the venetian blind, which faintly rustled like the little sound that balled-up paper makes when it relaxes in your wastebasket, and it was driving the doctor insane. "Fine! You send me Clarence," he said into the telephone. "I have a patient ready to be taken to A North. Right away, *please*." While they waited for Clarence to come and fetch Francis Rhinelander, the doctor got up, walked to the window, and shut it.

It was Dr. Erwin who, seven weeks later, signed Francis Rhinelander's release, citing a diagnosis of "temporary reactive psychosis" with the question of the stimulus to which the patient had been reacting, as is so often the case, left unanswered. At his hearing, the patient affirmed the reality of the music that he had hallucinated to be hallucinating. It was no strain for Francis to appear his naturally courteous and apologetic self, which had assured the three examining doctors, correctly, that he presented no danger to himself or others. The hospital had released him on his own recognizance.

Ida Farkasz

Ida Farkasz did not recognize her name being called, and the triage nurse had to come out into the waiting area and lead the patient into her office.

"Do you know where you are?" the nurse asked the patient.

"Where you are," said the patient and touched her forefinger to her lip, then to her chin, and then to her lip again.

The nurse spoke slowly into the patient's face. "Do. You. Know. Where. You. Live?"

Ida Farkasz frowned and said, "Where you live." Ida was frowning at not knowing what the person was saying to her. Not knowing had volume, was cloud-colored and located behind her eyes. Ida moved the finger from her lip to a place toward the back of the top of her head. She needed to put her hand inside, to reach around the way you reach around inside a drawer for—what?

The triage nurse had to walk the patient into the ER. "They'll take care of you! You sit here."

Ida sat on a chair and touched her lip, her chin.

The nurse went back out to the triage office and called Phyllis on the second floor.

Samson Gorewitz

Lucy saw Benedict. She watched him talking to a pleasant-looking nurse who had just come on duty.

"Yours is Samson Gorewitz," the nurse was saying, "the transfer from Glenshore General." The old man lay flat on his back and looked at the ceiling. Benedict had to lean over the gurney to place himself in the patient's field of vision, and he said,

"Hi! Hello. I'm your interviewer." Benedict asked the patient if he knew where he was and thought the old man said, "In heaven." He spoke out of the right corner of his mouth, which was raised and might be smiling. He said,

"Iftheyfindmenotlookintheotherplace."

Benedict experienced a powerful sense of ill usage: this was not what he had signed on for. He looked around for that pleasant nurse but she had her back to him, standing on tiptoe to write on the green chalkboard mounted high on the wall. Benedict looked to his mother, whose head was lowered over something she was writing on her lap. He wished himself back in the office, wanted his computer, but followed the orderly who had come to wheel his patient into one of the cubicles. It was like the cubicle where they had sat with his father; Benedict had stood because there was always only one chair. His mother had worried about it.

Benedict was alone with the old man the right side of whose face might be laughing.

"Name?" the Intake Form prompted Benedict to ask him.

The patient must be saying "Samson Gorewitz." It was typed in on the form.

"Social Security?"

The patient palpated the chest of the hospital gown,

which had no pocket, but the number, his birth information, and a Columbus, Ohio, street address were also typed on the appropriate lines.

"Nearest relative?" asked the Intake Form.

"Mysn Stewrt."

"Excuse me?"

"Mysn inpairs."

A son, was it, in pairs! Let that go for the moment.

"Marital status?"

Benedict made out that the patient was widowed.

"Education?"

"Hiostate."

"Ohio State? Is that right?"

"Ratrat!"

"Occupation?" Benedict was unable, first and last, to make out what the patient had done with, to, or about a "peppermill."

Next to "Comments," Benedict noted, One-sided facial paralysis (?) makes patient's speech difficult/impossible to follow. May be confused/demented (?)

Lucy saw Dr. Haddad approaching and raised her hand, and then lowered it to adjust her hair at the back when the doctor passed without stopping. It's what we do to keep the world from witnessing that we have been left standing on the sidewalk by an empty cab—the anti-Semite! Well, but hold on now: Haddad might be preserving the fiction that Lucy was like any regular patient, waiting to be attended to.

Lucy watched the doctor walk into the cubicle into which Benedict had followed the patient on the gurney, and out of which, in another moment, he emerged calling to the Pleasant Nurse: "The doctor wants you to get him a proper pillow." Lucy's eyes followed Benedict, who moved in the direction of the exit, where he passed the two old women hovering in the doorway.

Deborah and Shirley

Joe had praised Lucy's powers of observation. It had her wondering about the things she thought she knew about those two women. They were sisters; their four black eyes peered in with identical anxiety. They were expecting to learn certain hideous news. This cruel anxiety of theirs, however, was momentarily displaced by the little acute malaise of not knowing if they were allowed to just walk into the ER. Lucy beckoned to them: Come on! You can come on in. They stepped into the foreign space in which they did not know whether they were meant to move forward, to the left or right: They suspected themselves of being the wrong people in the wrong place, about to be found out. Lucy liked the one with the gray hair. The other had home-dyed her hair a black color that does not exist in nature; some sales lady had instructed her to tie the scarf like that. She didn't look like New York. The two women found the cubicle Benedict had come out of and went in.

Deborah and Shirley came through the curtains, which the young person with the—what do they call the thing they wear over their head?—parted for them. "You have visitors," she said to Sammy on the gurney.

They had to arrange their faces before they came and kissed the smiling half of his face, the half that looked like Sammy. The other, the left half, had suffered a slippage. Shirley covered her mouth with her hand.

Deb said, "Sammy, sweetheart! I'm furious with you! What made you go down that beach alone at five o'clock in the a.m.!"

"I didn't go by myself."

"What, sweetheart?" They did not understand what he said.

"I did *not* go by myself!"

They understood his shaking his head, "No."

"You did, too," Deb said, "because I spoke to the people at the Glenshore hospital and they picked you up all the way down on the beach and you were all alone."

Samson said, "I know, but that first morning, when I came down to breakfast, I sat in an empty seat. It turned out they were a family. The dad ..." Sam had to laugh. "He had on, it must have been the mom's hat with a big, floppy white brim, and he said, 'On your feet, everybody.' He didn't mean me, of course, but I tagged along behind the little boy, Charley. He didn't want to go and he was crying."

The two women listened with horror to what kept bubbling out of their brother's one-sided mouth. Samson said, "They go down for the day—towels, umbrella, big ball, sandwiches. I'd forgotten my sun lotion. When we were kids, didn't I always get burned? I knew I should turn over, I kept thinking I was going to turn over onto my stomach …"

"Is his speech going to come back?" Deborah asked the woman with the—the hijab is what they called it.

"We're surprised at the degree of language he has already recovered. Understanding him is a sort of trick, like finding the angle from which you can make out the figures in a holograph."

Sammy said, "When we were kids, did everybody squeal when they hit the water? I liked Joey and Stacey. They said 'Sorry!' for dripping on me when they came running out. They dripped on Charley purposely and made him cry."

"Can you find a vase for these?" Shirley thrust her bunch of multicolored flowers at the hijab, who would not take them from her.

"Sorry, we can't do flowers in the ER. I'm sorry."

"How do you mean you can't 'do' flowers?"

"Shirley, godsake," Deb said, "She's the *doctor*!"

Here's where Shirley registered the stethoscope around the neck of the white coat, but was *not* about to admit that she was embarrassed. "So?" she said, "Can't she just hand them to a nurse?"

"Since when do you ask doctors to do your flowers?" Deb pressed on. There are times when we go on talking as if certain other persons in the room with us will oblige us by not hearing or not understanding that we're arguing about them.

"Whatever," Shirley had learned from her grandchildren to say.

Samson said, "When Joey and Stacey went up the beach for ice cream they didn't wait for Charley and he cried and ran after them. Remember Stewy's little legs running? I meant to turn my head to watch Charley, but it didn't turn."

The hijab, so unpleasantly associated in Shirley's mind with her faux pas about the flowers, seemed not to be going to leave. She stood at the foot of Sammy's gurney. She was writing on his chart. She said, "His vitals are good."

"So are *you* his doctor?" Shirley asked her.

"I'm his doctor in the ER. We're finding Mr. Gorewitz a bed in our Senior Center, for rehab."

"Rehab? Oh, yes, I see. How long is he going to be in rehab?"

"Several weeks for sure. His vitals, as I say, are good but he may need to relearn to walk, and some personal skills. He'll get speech therapy." To the patient she said, "I'll be looking in on you. Enjoy your visitors."

When she was gone, Shirley said to Deb, "What do you hope to gain by being rude to Samson's doctors?"

"Doc*tors*? How many doc*tors* have I been rude to?"

"You would never ask a regular doctor to do your flowers."

Samson said, "She's Jewish," and they said, "Okay! It's okay, sweetheart!" and each took a hand and held it.

*

"What are you reading?" Phyllis from the second floor asked her granddaughter, who had been dropped off to spend the afternoon.

"A story," said the little girl.

Phyllis told her to take her book and sit at Bethy's desk. Bethy had gone down to the ER to interview Ida Farkasz. "What's the story all about?"

The granddaughter was reading a story about a girl who is so beautiful that the sun, which has seen everything, is amazed every time it shines into her face. The stepmother of the girl in the story is a witch who is mean and cruel to the girl. And where is the girl's father? He is gone away on business; he is gone hunting; he is, at any rate, away, and the girl runs away. She comes to a great, dark forest. When night falls she curls up in a hollow tree and goes to sleep, and Phyllis's granddaughter and Phyllis and Bethy Bernstine know, and Ida Farkasz used to know, and even people who have not read, and never been told the story, know that the girl will marry the prince with the kind eyes. They will inherit half the kingdom, and if they haven't died they are living to this hour.

Ida Farkasz

When Bethy walked into the ER, she saw Lucy and she saw the fat girl and the fat mother, who was telling the brother to quit already, and throw the bottle in the trash. That was when the legs of the old man with the blood dried on his forehead shot suddenly upward as if a puppeteer had decided the moment had come to pull all his strings at once.

"Is he okay?" Bethy asked.

"He's fine," the Mayan Nurse said.

"Which is Ida Farkasz?"

The nurse pointed to a sleeping hunchback and said, "Doesn't know *who* she is, where she lives, or anything. I'll see if there's a free cubicle. Going to be one of those nights."

Bethy said, "Ida Farkasz? I'm supposed to interview you."

The old person was not a hunchback. You see subway drunks, sometimes, who have descended into a sleep so deep it cancels the human instinct to remain sitting up in a public place. The old woman had slipped way down the seat of her chair. Her gray head with its pinkish patches of scalp was curled forward onto her diminished, child-sized breast. There are things—and may we forgive ourselves that there are people—we would rather not touch. Bethy Bernstine placed her right forefinger on this old person's sleeve. "Mrs. Farkasz?" she said, and Ida opened her eyes and turned the corners of her mouth so radically downward that Bethy thought, She doesn't like me.

Bethy sat across from the dreadful old person and asked her did she know where she was.

"The Emergency Room, Cedars of Lebanon."

"Name?"

"Ida Farkasz."

"Do you know where you live?"

Ida Farkasz named her New York address and the date and place of her birth: "Pojorny before World War One, when it was still Hungary. The Slovaks call it Bratislava. In German it's Pressburg."

The Intake Form for Seniors had no rubric for the twentieth-century history of the Austro-Hungarian Empire. "Nearest relative?"

"Marta, my daughter. My sister Poldi and I don't talk."

"You remember your daughter's phone number?"

"And a lot of good it does me. I call and have my little chat with the answering machine and then I sit on a chair in my apartment and wait for it to occur to my daughter to call me back."

"Marital status?"

"Some status," said Ida Farkasz, "when your new husband takes you home from the wedding on the bus with a carpet rolled under his arm."

"A carpet? How do you mean 'carpet'?"

"Carpet! A carpet. Crappy thing that Mama had by her bed and *Berta* thought I might use in my *foyer.* Who had a *foyer*? Berta was the oldest so *she* got the apartment at Twelve Judengasse. In the end, of course, the Nazis got it. Poldi and Kari, and Miklos and I were the only ones that got out. Who brings *a carpet* to a wedding?"

"Occupation?"

"The Nazis marched into Bratislava in March of 1939 . . . ?"

"I think they mean *your* occupation—what work did you do?"

"Miklos was dead by the time the child and I got to New York. Poldi had a job as companion to her 'Miss *Margate*.' Never introduced me, never took me to Miss Margate's '*evenings*.' Didn't take me with her to Herta Frankel's birthday, and it wasn't even Poldi, it was *me* that was in Herta's class, even if we weren't best friends."

"What work did *you* do?"

"Poldi's Kari used to import wine in Bratislava, with a branch in Vienna. In New York, the men got jobs as mail clerks. *Packerl Schupfer*, we used to call them. 'Little-parcel-tossers.' After he died—that was Fifty-three—Marta and I moved in with Poldi and I got my social work certificate and worked at the Kastel House Social Security office where *no one* told me and *no one* told Herbie Dukazs what courses you were meant to take for promotion."

"Social worker," wrote Bethy on the line on the Intake Form for Seniors.

"In the end, Herbie decided to move back to Budapest. He made me pay him thirty-five dollars for his bed—never mind that it was I had sewed the bedcover for him! I borrowed Poldi's Miss Margate's Singer sewing machine. He said that's what the fabric alone cost him, which maybe it did. One lousy postcard that he sent me from his vacation on Balatonlelle."

"Education?" asked the Intake Form.

"Poldi's Kari had something on the ball," said Ida Farkasz. "He got them to New York, illegally, via Canada, while

Miklos and the child and I sat in the Hotel Budapest in Santo Domingo, waiting for our '*quota.*' He had a little Hitler mustache, Miklos. Listen," Ida Farkasz told Bethy Bernstine, "a woman remembers her husband taking her home from her wedding on the bus."

Lucy

Nurse Trotwood brought Lucy a gown and said, "It ties at the back."

Lucy said, "I think I'm supposed to wait for Dr. Haddad."

Trotwood said, "You'll put your clothes in this bag." The bag was large and said PATIENTS PROPERTY in black capitals on the outside, and the missing possessive apostrophe is to be understood to remain a subliminal irritation in Lucy's mind for the rest of this novel. Lucy remembered that she was meant to act like a regular patient, and followed the nurse.

Each cubicle had a single wall and three sides formed by a blue curtain attached to a circular rail set into the ceiling. This one looked like—it might *be* the cubicle in which they had sat and watched Bertie die. There'd been no chair for Benedict to sit on. Benedict had been irritable with her.

There had to have been a designer, a person, who

designed the curtain to be blue. Lucy thought this person had meant well, meant blue because it's a pleasant color, but this blue was stained by pain, the fear of pain, of watching pain.

Lucy put on the cotton gown, its blue pinstripes leached out by institutional laundering. She folded her own clothes into the bag. The chair was hard, so Lucy climbed onto the gurney and sat there till the nurse came to take her blood pressure. It was the Pleasant Nurse with a nice face and the low voice that people like King Lear thought to be a good thing in a woman. "Your hands are the same temperature as my arm," Lucy said to her. The Pleasant Nurse was not a chatterer nor a smiler. The patience in her face, Lucy thought, came not of suffering but of natural goodness. Her cheek, at close quarters, was like Lucy's mother's cheek, which had received the impression of Lucy's kiss, returning, when her lips lifted away, to its soft convexity. Were my cheeks soft for Benedict? For Bertie? "Toward the end we had to keep rushing my husband here to Emergency," Lucy said to the nurse, who was winding the blood-pressure sleeve into an efficient roll. She said, "The doctor will be in to see you," and went softly away.

Lucy sat on the gurney. From inside here she could observe nothing. Would Dr. Haddad know where she was? Lucy wanted a book the way a drunk wants his liquor. Lucy proposed to herself to eyeball every object within her view: One chair. Industrial-size garbage can, khaki. Sink with knee handle. Purity Hand Sanitizer. Two gadgets plugged into outlets with black plastic nozzles of different designs for insertion, was it, into differently shaped orifices? Cartoon chart to identify pain by degrees from smiley face to face with down-turned mouth and falling teardrops. On the white-painted metal cabinet was tacked a paper listing contents. Words to read: Alcohol pads, Culturettes gc/Chlamydia, Probes pink/blue, Hemoccult cards, Developer, Surgilube Towelettes, Chuxs. (!?) Chuxs sterile 2x2's sterile 4x4's Gloves 6 size 6½ NS (500cc) with IV. FOLD GOWNS NEATLY.

Lucy lay down on the gurney. Lucy sat up. Lucy got off the gurney and hunted through PATIENTS PROPERTY for her handbag, found her pen, took her reading glasses out of their case, turned her address book to the empty Y page, and wrote,

> *I was wrong: I'm not posting outward into the expanding universe. I'm lying on a shelf. On a Monday, last October, you walk into your office and I'm on your desk. You call the intern—Bennington literature major on work program, smart as they come. You tell her, "Read this and do me a one-paragraph critique." Intern carries me out to the reception desk, reads "Rumpelstiltskin in Emergency" which may be the greatest thing she has read in her "entire" life, except that she doesn't "really" know—i.e., hasn't an idea—what it's supposed to be about . . .*

Lucy saw she was going to run out of space and reduced her writing to the size of the letters in a miniature book in a dollhouse library.

. . . She slides me to the corner of her desk for another read the next day but Tuesday you give her two essays and a batch of poems and Wednesday another story until your regular girl returns. Before Bennington leaves she piles the manuscripts, with "Rumpelstiltskin" at the bottom, on the shelf in your office.

Francis Rhinelander

In the cubicle to Lucy's right, Francis Rhinelander never stopped tugging at the too-short hospital gown. Al looked down the Intake Form. "Precipitating Factor?"

"Blacked out in the lobby of my hotel," said the old man. "My brother made me go for a checkup this morning, before I got on the train. And I guess I forgot to have breakfast?"

Francis had carried his overnighter across Godford Memorial Hospital's half-empty parking lot and the thought of something being found to be a little bit the matter with him and getting put to bed in one of Memorial's quiet rooms was not unpleasant. The front desk stood in a square of sun that outlined Angie Biddle, the receptionist, with a faintly furred halo of light. Angie had gone to school with the Rhinelander boys. "George called in," she told Francis. "He wants us to take a look at you before you head back to town."

"Am I going to make the eleven twenty-five?"

Angie thought he surely would. "The nurse practitioner gets in at ten. Take a load off." She pointed to the chair beside her.

Francis said, "George was telling me Margaret West died? *You* took piano with her."

Angie said, "Margaret sang at my wedding. Remember the plaque they gave her for the song they got her to write for the Godford Two-Hundredth Independence parade? I think it embarrassed her. She didn't think it was that good of a song."

"It was okay," remembered Francis. "I was the drum down Main Street."

The Godford marching band had followed behind the fire engine driven at a walking pace by Fred Willis, the chief of the volunteer fire department, with the mayor sitting beside him. They halted across from the cannon with the seven black cannonballs stacked in a pyramid on the grass triangle where Main met High Street. The public, which barely outnumbered the marchers, stood or sat. Babies crawled on the grass and dogs sniffed for treats while the town notables spelled each other in the reading of the Declaration of Independence. "I used to wait for the wicked king and the vicious Indians," Francis told Angie. "And did you wonder what a sacred honor was exactly, and if you had one?"

Angie didn't remember wondering anything.

"Margaret West!" mused Francis. "When I was fifteen she'd pass on her younger students for me to teach."

"Up and died," Angie said.

The nurse practitioner walked in and Angie Biddle

told him, "This is Mr. Rhinelander. Francis, you go along with him."

"You think I can make the eleven twenty-five?" Francis asked the nurse, who said, "No problem." He was a stout, youngish man with a ponytail and a mustache so orange that Francis had to take another look and kept looking. He said, "My brother worries about me?" and the nurse, though it was not clear in reference to what, said that it was no problem and asked if Mr. Rhinelander had remembered not to have breakfast. Rhinelander had eaten no breakfast. The nurse took enough of Francis's blood to fill several glass vials, each one stoppered with a different-colored rubber stopper and labeled with Francis's name. The nurse asked Francis how he was feeling. Francis said he had felt funny at dinner last night, but did not tell this stranger with the orange mustache that he'd sat next to his sister-in-law, Sybil, whose perfume-like candied roses had got into the chowder on his plate and Francis had had to rise in a hurry and said would anybody mind if he went and just lay down. He went and lay down on the sofa in the living room where George's boys' music played day in day out.

When the nurse said, "You're good to go," Francis continued to sit. Standing up seemed an improbability.

"You want Angie to phone Willis Cabs for you?"

"Oh, no. No, thank you." Rhinelander rose.

"Now you make sure you eat something. You have your doctor in New York? He can call us for the results."

It was past two in the afternoon by the time Francis Rhinelander became part of the crowd on the move under Grand Central Terminal's midnight sky where the spheres are outlined into figures, properly labeled, of the zodiac. The music came from a brass band ranged in rows before the marble stairs. A little boy sat on a chair next to the trombonist's chair. The trombonist blew into his trombone; the boy blew into his straw, which made the milk bubble in his glass.

How was it that Rhinelander's urgent, his repeated finger on the *Off* button of the taxi's little TV screen kept turning the music *on*? He considered appealing to the driver, the back of whose flattened head attached without the mediation of a neck to his hulking back; he looked like something by Charles Addams. Francis sat with his right hand holding on to his left.

Francis Rhinelander's letter to the residence hotel's management arguing for a lobby minus music had gone unanswered and those merry violins messed with his disordered stomach. "I didn't have any breakfast," Francis had told the desk clerk, a man of his own age, who advised Mr. Rhinelander to leave his bag and see if the Café's kitchen wouldn't rustle him up a bite of something.

"Frank Sinatra was singing 'New York New York,' " Rhinelander complained to Al Lesser.

Al said, "My nana once *met* Frank Sinatra," and blushed.

"I'm always asking them to turn it off," Francis said, "and they say the patrons like the music."

But this had been after lunch and before dinner. There was nobody except the wait staff sitting down to their own meal in the back. Rhinelander's waiter was that little man, elderly, with an accent, who had to put his knee up on a chair to reach the button. Rhinelander told Al, "They'll turn Frank Sinatra down—but never off and afterward the volume always goes back up a little and a little. I think it's they can't be without music?"

Young Al mentally patted the iPod in his pocket. On it, he had his Norah Jones, his Black Keys, Jay-Z, Manu Chao, Adele, and Lady Gaga. He said, "But you're a composer! You taught piano. You don't like music?"

"Not in my mushroom omelet!" cried Francis. "I left the tip and I walked out." It had seemed cruelly unfair to Francis that Frank Sinatra and the whole band pursued him into the john. But it was the violins, when he went to pick up his overnighter, that finally floored him. The old clerk must have been on his break. The chunky woman in a navy outfit like a uniform was saying, "Sir? Sir, are you okay, sir?" as Francis reached for the edge of the desk, which moved away at a fantastically increasing speed down a perspective like the small end of a telescope.

"Sir?"

Francis took one step and another before that last little hop after which nothing was going to keep the floor from slapping him in the face.

"Do you need medical attention?" asked the woman in the uniform, and the two men who stepped out of the elevator and saw the always-surprising length of a body facedown on the floor, skipped in the direction of the door, which revolved them out into the avenue.

The woman in the uniform had phoned 911 for the ambulance, which brought Francis Rhinelander to the Cedars of Lebanon's ER.

In the other cubicle sat Deb and Shirley holding their brother's hands. Deborah said, "Sweetheart, you'll be in rehab for just a bit, okay? You'll be fine! You'll come out and I'll put a bed in the den, nice and private for you, okay?"

"Thegravesafineandprivateplace," Samson said.

"What does he want?" Deb and Shirley asked each other.

Samson Gorewitz

On the late afternoon beach, the sun had not been a factor, no longer burning directly down on Samson's upturned face and exposed chest and legs.

They were packing up, collecting their things. Stacey and Joey, who were supposed to fold the big towel, kept yanking the corners out of each other's hands, and laughing.

"Kids, kids! Come on!"

They collapsed the umbrella. Who was going to carry it?

"I'm not carrying the umbrella!"

"*I* will carry the umbrella." The dad's voice.

Who said, "I didn't bring the ball so no way am I going to carry it."

"Who brought the ball?"

"You said to bring the ball. You carry the ball." They were moving away. Stacey was back for whatever it was that Charley had been supposed to carry. Charley was crying.

Samson listened. They were gone? The rolled-up shirt under his neck barely tilted his head so that Samson's view was empty sky.

Little Stewy had asked his dad, "How do you do the sky?" The boy was drawing a seascape—ocean with waves, boat with sail, and a sun with rays in the white paper gap between the blue of the ocean and the blue sky he had crayoned along the top edge of the paper: Stewy knew that wasn't right and he asked, "How far down does the sky come?" His father said, "Why sweet boy, you know heaven is everywhere around you." But it wasn't. Stewy put out his hand and it did not meet any blue, and there was no white paper.

That evening Samson lay on the beach, on his back, looked upward into the golden blue air, and thought about Stewy's question.

He knew there were people behind him and that they were passing from left to right. The air cooled unpleasantly on his heated flesh.

A little boy jumped over Samson's legs. He wore navy swim trunks with tiny white whales. The boy ran back and jumped again. The father and mother looked back and told him to "Stop it and say sorry to the gentleman."

"I can't move," Sam said to the child, who saw saliva bubble out of the grown man's mouth and ran after his parents and pulled on their hands to make them keep walking.

There was a star to look at. Sam looked at it. There was a second star, a number of stars.

"I can't move," he meant to shout up the bare young legs like slim young trees that multiplied into a running forest past his right side. All night Sam was going to feel the ghost of the spray of sand he couldn't lift his hand to brush from the corner near his eye. The girl had looked down, hesitated—would have stopped if the man's hand, interlocked with hers, had not drawn her onward into the waves, which were suddenly right here. Samson thought, I'm going to drown. It was the first but not the only time in the night on the empty beach that his upturned face crumpled, and the tears, having nowhere to flow off, collected in his eye and fractured his vision like the rain on a windshield.

He resented the chill, and having nothing to cover him.

Samson was going to cheat boredom, going to chart the blue air's incremental darkening and graying. Samson meant to watch change happen, but he kept forgetting to watch, and the gray was blacker, was already black, nor did Sam, lying on his back on the empty beach, ever once catch change in the act.

His piece of heaven was peppered with the stars which he had never cared to know by name and they did nothing, now, to entertain him. The first wave licked his foot to the ankles and retired. He waited for the next assault, waited, waited, waited. The shock of the wet cold on sun-cooked flesh had been unpleasant. For the second time he wept. The next wave shocked him by lapping his knee, retreated and immediately returned. Help me! Had he been able to turn his head he could have looked for the girl with the running legs and the man. In which direction had they gone? Disappeared? Was he alone on the expanse of the night beach to his right and left?

Help me!

It never got so black that the small clouds didn't show a deeper black. The cold wet slapped and kept slapping his groin. You cannot, it turns out, panic for hours on end. Later he thought nothing and must have slept because he woke drowning, swallowing, coughing water, opened his mouth to shout and swallowed more water and drowned again and again.

Samson Gorewitz lay in exquisite discomfort, radically chilled, exhausted, without expectations on the empty beach. Off and on he wept and did not care to know how the sky lightened incrementally to gray to silver.

The jogger ran way down the beach along the wavelets that looked to have been drawn by a lovingly sharpened pencil. Serene and limpid, they magnified a string of seaweed, the convolutions of a shell whose inhabitant had moved on. The horizon was beginning to spray needles of light into the chilly air, which was a funny time for the fat old codger with the shirt rolled under his neck, wide-legged old-codger swim trunks, to be napping like something the high tide had deposited. The jogger wondered, as he did every morning, with no intention of researching the explanation, why the morning's first light is so purely white and what chemistry introduces the golden adulteration of the later hours. He ran on but kept turning to look where the fat man lay on his back in the sand with a stillness not of inanimate objects and not of sleep. The jogger reversed direction.

But the fat old man's eyes were open in intelligent terror. The right side of his mouth bubbled saliva. "I can't move!" Samson Gorewitz thought he said to the sudden human leaning out of the blare of white light.

One two three. He felt himself lifted, he lay on a white bed that moved him swiftly, moved him smoothly away. White figures, male and female, surrounded, bending to him. Samson could not contain the broad smile he knew himself to be helplessly smiling in the bliss of being warm, of being dry.

Glenshore General stabilized the patient. From the information found in the wet wallet in the breast pocket of his wet shirt, they notified a sister living in the city. They transferred the patient to the better facilities of Cedars of Lebanon.

Lucy

Had Dr. Haddad given the order for Lucy to be wheeled back into the general area to continue her observation, or was it to make room for the gurney, its sides up, in which a broken young black man lay with closed eyes? His girl walked alongside carrying his brown bomber jacket over her arm.

"Don't even try to undress him," Dr. Haddad told the Pleasant Nurse before the curtains closed around them.

"What happened to him?" Lucy asked the nurse, when she came out a few minutes later.

"You don't want to know," the Pleasant Nurse said, and hurried on her way.

Here there were things to read that somebody, at a point in time, had tacked up on the weight-bearing column by Lucy's left elbow, and which it had never been anybody's business to take down. Lucy read every word of every notice, including the printer's miniature identification on the lower left: Lists, memoranda, warnings. She took her time studying the picture postcard of a blue, blue ocean. Lucy and Bertie had honeymooned in the Bahamas, where the water was this postcard-ocean blue. Christmas kittens with poinsettias; a snapshot of someone's actual cat; a toddler in a Bo Peep bonnet who might by now be entering kindergarten, or graduating high school. A group photo of blue-striped nurse's aides smiling in unison. They'd taken Benedict to

Washington for his graduation and the corridor behind the Supreme Court was lined with the annual group photos of the robed justices, front row seated, back row standing. Bertie had identified the first year the photographer told the Supreme Court to say cheese. Funny man, Bertie.

Lucy looked left, for the young woman who had been crying. Had she fallen asleep?

Lucy looked for things to observe. The wall had shelves with files. The tabs made a color pattern. Might these files contain whatever it was that she was meant to be finding out? Lucy understood that she was not going to climb down from her gurney with the gown opening down her back; that she was not going to take the several steps to those shelves, was not going to take down or read any one of all these files.

Lucy could imagine Maurie not reading any of the manuscripts accumulated on the shelf in his office.

What was the Mayan Nurse writing on the green chalkboard?

"What do the numbers after the names mean?" Lucy asked her.

The Mayan Nurse stopped writing, turned to look for the source of the voice, looked at Lucy: "What do you mean, 'numbers'?" she said, turned back to add a comma, more numbers, and then she hurried toward Dr. Stimson who looked like Lucy's tax man. He was calling her.

Lucy picked up the clipboard that lay on the sheet over her legs but Trotwood, happening by, swiped it out of her grasp and attached it to the foot of Lucy's gurney, out of

Lucy's reach. "Why can't I read what it says on my clipboard?" Lucy asked, but Trotwood went on her way.

The relief of something happening, even if it was only the resistance of the wheels of Lucy's gurney to being shifted sideways to make barely enough room for the gurney with the crooked old person. Without her glasses she glared at Lucy out of marvelous black eyes. She said, "Somebody must have said something to Herta because she said I could come if I wanted. I said, 'No, thank you,' and she said, 'Come on, I'm asking you, aren't I?' I said, 'Maybe I don't want to even go to your party?' I thought, If she asks me, properly, I'll go, and she said, 'You can come, if you want,' which was not asking properly, so I said, 'I told you, I don't even want to,' and she said, 'Please yourself,' and she didn't ask me again. Poldi went to the party and she wasn't even *in* the same class as Herta. Poldi never took me up to Miss Margate's apartment."

Lucy wanted her to stop talking so she could make out what the excitable little square woman was saying in a language so congested with consonants that Lucy did not immediately recognize it as English. The ancient woman she pushed in the wheelchair wore an admirably tailored suit, had the true white hair, major nose. The retreat of flesh had exposed a fine jaw.

"Anstiss Adams!" The doctor with the good young hair was coming to take her hand. "You're becoming a habit! Luba, what happened?"

"She hit again the head!"

"Do not do not do not tell me what I hit."

"She hit on the stairs!"

"Get me that gurney over there," the doctor said, "and we'll take a look at the head."

"She has hidden my shoes."

Lucy climbed out of the pit, in which somebody was shouting. She opened her eyes and here was Benedict, and somebody was shouting.

"I just closed my eyes." Lucy didn't want him to feel that he had woken her up.

"I just walked in!" Benedict didn't want her to feel that she had kept him standing. "Did you find out anything? *Is* there anything *to* find out?"

"Are you supposed to know me?"

"My god! A son visits his mother in the ER. Have you met up with the Haddad?"

"Benedict, do you remember when Dad and I took you to Washington, and we went to the Supreme Court?"

"Washington? Sure. Mom, did anything happen?"

"Just that they won't explain the numeric code on the green chalkboard. What does it say next to my name?"

"Looks like today's date and the time of your admission. Why is that man shouting?"

"And they won't let me see what is written on my clipboard."

"Let's take a look. Blood pressure: one-thirty over seventy-five, which is good, isn't it? Temperature ninety-eight is good. You're breathing okay. Mom, listen: Joe says, when you check out in the morning, stay in the waiting area. He wants to debrief you before he checks himself in. He's decided to hold the meeting with the hospital people in the cafeteria. The latest bee in his bonnet is to imagine that a public space would be harder to bug than Haddad's office. Oh! Hello!" Benedict said to the beautiful Dr. Miriam Haddad.

"Hello," the doctor said. "And how are you making out?" she asked Lucy.

"Why is that man shouting?" Benedict asked the doctor.

Dr. Miriam Haddad was looking to the door, where more patients were entering the ER, and asked the orderly to start wheeling gurneys out into the adjoining corridors. "If you know any rich friends who would like to donate us an adequate new ER, send them right along."

"Where are you taking me!" screamed Ida Farkasz.

"Miss, just right outside the door," said the orderly.

"Why does she get to stay?" howled the little crooked person, and she glared at Lucy.

Anstiss Adams had been sedated and was blessedly asleep, and they asked Luba to go and sit out in the waiting area. Samson Gorewitz's sisters were asked to leave and come back in the morning to visit their brother over in the Senior Center's rehab.

"Why can't they sedate him?" Benedict scrunched up his eyes against the shouting from the cubicle at the other side of the ER; it had taken on the character of a bellow.

Dr. Haddad said, "The head wound gone around the bend."

"Can't they give him something?"

"Not till Dr. Stimson has seen him—who, by the way, wants to attend your meeting."

Benedict said, "Which is going to take place in the cafeteria. That sound is unendurable ..."

"The sound," Dr. Haddad said, "of someone enduring the unendurable. You'll have to excuse me." She went to join a large number of the staff collecting in the cubicle from which the bellowing must be imagined to issue for the rest of the night.

"I can't believe they can't give him *something*!" Benedict said. Lucy told him to go home. "Go on, really. Give my love to Gretel. And I'll see you in the morning."

"You have your cell?"

"Except they won't let me use it in the ER. Benedict, go *home*!"

Luba

In the waiting area, on his way out, Benedict passed another commotion. The triage nurse had already reported "Patient around the bend" and sent for backup. The overflow waiting-room population watched the young security guard failing to prevent the sturdy little Luba from removing the last piece of her underclothes. He held the jacket of his uniform around her, attempting to keep it closed over the breasts that hung like flattened gourds and the interesting stomach fold, simultaneously hiding the square buttocks without having himself to come in contact with any part of so much pink elderly flesh.

Morning in the ER

Morning in the ER, the technology becalmed, telephones and computers stilled. The man with the head wound, who had bellowed through the night, must be asleep or dead. The little crooked Ida, the young woman who had cried, the vomiting fat girl, the unusually tall old man with the sweet, smashed face, the ancient Anstiss who had gone around the bend—had they been taken care of? And the broken, black young man and his girl? Lucy would never know what became of them.

The Mayan Nurse and the Pleasant Nurse were leaving but stopped to softly squeal with the day nurse coming on duty: Shareen had a little boy! Seven and a half pounds, twenty-two inches. The two night nurses left. The day nurse walked toward Lucy, and Lucy said, "I have to go to the bathroom."

The nurse tacked a snapshot of a newborn onto the column by Lucy's elbow. She said, "When I get my coat off," and walked out of sight and did not return.

Lucy slid off the gurney to be waylaid by Trotwood

with her handbag already over her shoulder. She told Lucy, "You don't go getting off your gurney by yourself!"

"I'm looking for a bathroom."

"Well, you don't get off your gurney."

"I called. Nobody came."

"Get back on your gurney, please," said Trotwood and she, too, went home.

Benedict called the office. "Has my mom come in?"

"What d'you mean? She's in the ER," said Al.

"Only she *isn't.* Joe and I are here, in the waiting area. I *told* Lucy he wanted to talk to her before he checked himself in. The nurses didn't know that she'd checked out. The release officer hasn't seen her. She didn't go home, because I've been calling. So listen. Joe is going to check in and we won't schedule the meeting with Dr. Stimson and the Haddads till we know when he's likely to get out. If Lucy comes into the office or calls, tell her to call me, or, Al, *you* call me!"

"Sure."

III
The Cafeteria

Lucy

Lucy checked her mailbox downstairs and there was nothing from Maurie, and went up to her apartment, and there was nothing on the answering machine except a couple of messages from Benedict: "Hi, Mom. Did you forget Joe wanted to debrief you before he checked himself in? Why didn't you wait for him in the waiting area? Call me."

Her phone rang. Lucy did not pick up. "Mom? Mom! Mom, call me when you get this message."

Lucy spent the morning in her study. Two shelves of published books. The file of all her unpublished work she transferred to PATIENTS PROPERTY.

The phone was ringing. "Mom?"

Lucy did not pick up.

When Benedict called around noon and got a busy signal, he was relieved: His mother must be home. He called again ten minutes later and must have just missed her. He left another message on her answering machine.

Lucy lugged PATIENTS PROPERTY up the two flights of stairs to the modest offices of *The Magazine*. The old broken-backed couch smelled of mold, but the girl was new. Maurie was not in and not expected. No, thanks, Lucy wouldn't leave a message. Thank you, there was nothing Lucy was going to leave.

She carried the bag down the stairs and took a cab to Maurie's. His daughter, Shari, answered the door. "Dad's in Saint Petersburg with a bunch of writers and people."

"Writers and people, of course. In Saint Petersburg. Your mother went with him?"

"Mom? Good god no. Mom wouldn't be caught dead on one of Daddy's junkets. The darling is giving me the afternoon off. Took both kids to little George Cameron's birthday party." Shari pointed across the street.

"And how old is … ?"

"Max is going on six, in kindergarten. Cassy turned three."

"Six! In kindergarten! Shari," said Lucy, "do you have any memories of our summers on Shelter Island? *You* were six and Benedict was all of three and fell into the sixteen-foot goldfish pond?"

"I do! I remember the baby wrapped in a big old towel and people telling me it wasn't my fault, which had never occurred to me! You want to sit down?"

"For just a moment."

"Coffee?"

"No no no no. Thanks."

"How *is* Benedict?"

"Fine. Good. Living with his Viennese girl. I like Gretel. Did you know Benedict and I are colleagues, working in the same office?"

"Cool!"

"Shari, you remember the Bernstines—Joe and Jenny? They were away for years running the Concordance Institute in Connecticut?"

"Sure. With a daughter who was angry at everything and everybody?"

"Still is. Poor Bethy. Curious, isn't it, how we used to live in each other's pockets! How do friends get divorced?"

Shari said, "Did you know I divorced Alex?"

Did I know that? wondered Lucy. "That's sad."

"Yes, well," said Shari, "not really."

Lucy knew that a single mom with children six and three must be wanting to have her free afternoon to herself. "I remember I'd throw Benedict a ball and think, I have my head to myself for the time it takes him to run, retrieve the ball, and roll it back to me …"

"Yes!" said Shari and laughed. "Yes, yes!"

"What apartment number did you say the birthday party was at?"

"The apartment number?"

"Of the birthday party. What's the number of the apartment?"

"The Camerons' apartment? It's Eleven-B."

"Dear Shari, lovely to see you, really it is!" The two women, the old one and the young one, embraced.

"Somebody at the door for you," the birthday boy's mother said to little Max's grandmother.

"Can't be. Who knows I'm here?"

"She's asking for you."

"Who is?" Ulla followed Eileen Cameron into the foyer where the woman standing in the door with the birthday party rampaging and hallooing around her would have been Lucy Friedgold if Lucy could be imagined to be standing in the Camerons' foyer holding a very large plastic bag. The bag had weight, judging from the angle at which her body leaned to create the counterbalance.

"Hello, Ulla," said Lucy. "Shari said I'd find you here."

"Oh, I see," said Ulla, but didn't.

"Is there somewhere we might talk?"

The birthday boy's mother said, "The magician is about to do his thing." It puzzled her good manners: Was it the hostess's business to welcome the elderly newcomer with the oversize bag who was advancing into her foyer, or was she supposed to protect little Max's grandmother from her?

"This won't take five minutes." With the hand that was not holding the bag, the intruder opened a random door. It happened to lead into the dining room. The table was covered with crimson crinkle-paper, slices of ruined chocolate cake on clown-face paper plates, birthday candles with blackened wicks, blasted party favors, rags of exploded balloons. The old woman with the bag seated herself on one of the dining chairs, obliging Max's grandmother to sit down also. "Five minutes, I promise!" The urbane smile, a certain distinction of face and dress partly reassured Eileen Cameron; she walked out but left the door open.

Lucy and Ulla had a clear view of the magician in a purple shirt and comical green tie that hung to his knees. He said, "Is there anybody here who can count to ten?"

"Me-e-e," shouted the little boys and girls.

The magician said, "Everybody, all together: One. Two. Three. Thursday. Friday. Saturday …"

"No-o-o!" shouted the children: The magician, who was a grown-up, had made a mistake! That was funny!

"That's the days of the week," a girl in a frilly blue dress explained to him.

"Oops!" The magician hit himself on the forehead.

Lucy said, "I sent Maurie the story I wrote after Bertie died, which Maurie has neither accepted nor rejected. It's called 'Rumpelstiltskin in Emergency.' "

"Maurie is in Saint Petersburg," Ulla said.

"Try again! Everybody, all together," the magician said: "One. Two. Three. April. May. June …"

"I sent it to him in October," Lucy said. "This is July!"

The children were laughing. It broke them up: The magician had made another mistake! Only the child in the blue frills frowned.

"Those are the *months* of the *year*!" she told him. She walked toward the magician, who hit himself on the forehead.

"Another Oops! Anybody counting the oopses? What's your name?" he asked the little girl. Her name was Jennifer.

"Lucy!" Ulla said, "What do you want from me?"

"I want you to give this to Maurie." Lucy hoisted PATIENTS PROPERTY onto Ulla's lap—surprising, always, the weight of paper.

"Christ, Lucy! Send it to him at *The Magazine*!"

"Which neither accepts, nor rejects, Ulla! Which doesn't so much as acknowledge receipt."

"Would somebody come up here and hold my magic stick for me?" The magician held the instrument high out of little Jennifer's reach. "Birthday boy, I need you to come right up here. Tell everybody your name."

"George," said the blissful child.

"George is going to hold my magic stick for me, but not like *that*! Hold it straight!" But that stick kept folding away from the little boy, who laughed. All the girls and boys laughed their high, happy, silver laughter and wriggled and got up and sat down and got up again, except for Jennifer who said, "*You're* doing that." She turned the giant green tie around to expose a pack of cards! A nest of little balls! A white mouse, and the fraudulent string! "You were pulling this!" Jennifer accused the magician, who whipped his tie smartly out of her hand and said, "Do we have any jugglers?"

"Me-e-e," shouted all the children.

"Lucy! Who acknowledges receipt? Who has the staff? Remember Freddy Wells saying publishing *The Reader* is like having a retarded child that's never going to grow up, is never going to take itself off your mind?"

"Freddy Wells! A sweet man," Lucy said. "Haven't seen Freddy in—I don't know how long! Does Freddy still say 'Ah, well,' as if it were a sigh?"

"Who can keep two balls in the air at the same time?" asked the magician.

Lucy said, "Shari and I were remembering Shelter Island. Croquet, Scrabble. What a lot of cooking everybody used to do."

Ulla said, "And in every room there was always somebody writing something. What was the name of the old pest—the old poet—who used to call and read Maurie her latest in the middle, always, of a dinner party—Olivia . . . ?"

"Liebeskind," said Lucy. "Olivia Liebeskind!"

"Didn't Maurie publish the story you wrote about her . . ."

" 'The Poet on the Telephone,' " said Lucy. "She wasn't a bad poet."

"Maurie says it isn't bad writing that's the problem, it's the perfectly good writing that never stops coming down the pike."

"A nightmare!" said Lucy. "What time is it? I have a meeting in the Cedars of Lebanon cafeteria." The two old friends kissed each other good-bye. Lucy picked up PATIENTS PROPERTY, called, "Thank you so much!" to the birthday boy's mother, and went out the door.

The cafeteria had been done over. It had been reconfigured into a horseshoe-shaped food court with ethnic food bars since Lucy had sat here with her cup of coffee and her sandwich waiting for them to bring Bertie back from a test, from another procedure, a procedure gone wrong that had to be done over. Not to worry, said the doctor, We do two or three of these a day. Sometimes Benedict sat with her.

Lucy tried to identify the table at which she had sat writing "Rumpelstiltskin." Curious not to be able to figure out in which direction she had faced. She was early, was the first. None of the Compendium people had arrived, neither had the Haddads. Lucy didn't know Salman Haddad by sight and couldn't, for the moment, remember the Chief of Emergency's name. She used PATIENTS PROPERTY to bag a table large enough for their number before going to find something to eat.

Where there are so many choices, you tend to eat what you always eat. Lucy got a cup of coffee and a cheese sandwich and sat down and watched the couple standing and waiting for the short Mexican waitress—she was hardly taller than a dwarf—to wipe down the table for them. He held the tray, she carried his jacket. What was it about them that told Lucy the patient they had come to visit was close to neither—her aunt, maybe, or his elderly cousin; that they had decided, without the need for discussion, to eat before getting back into their car? Lucy was never going to cross the space between herself and them to ask, "Excuse me, but am I correct in being so certain that you are in your late fifties and you're not Manhattanites?" Her certainties were reinforced entirely by her certainties.

She watched them eat in silence, their eyes on their plates. What was there to see in each other's faces, or to say that had not been seen or said long ago, and often? He lowered his head to shorten the spoon's passage from the bowl to his mouth. Escarole and bean soup from the Italian Bar.

"Taste?" she asked him.

"Hm," he said, and opened his mouth into which she guided a careful forkful of pasta in tomato.

"Hmm," he said.

The apple pie, not from the Italian Bar, they ate with two forks from the same dish; she took care to leave him the larger half.

The short Mexican—*was* she a Mexican?—was clearing a table for a stout black dad in a business suit and his boy dressed in his best—not, hoped Lucy, to appease a sick mom. The dad took out a cell phone and dialed. The boy dripped ketchup on a fry in the front, a fry in the back, and this fry, and that one, creating a ketchup loop before picking up his burger. The dad finished his call, helped himself to one of the boy's fries, and dialed another number.

Two blond young people moved the dishes from their two trays onto the table and took out their BlackBerrys.

The father finished his second call and asked the boy if he was going to want ice cream. The boy said, no, he didn't. The dad was looking for a number on his cell, found it and dialed, a business call this, a professional laugh. The boy changed his mind. He wanted ice cream. When he returned with—it looked like vanilla and chocolate—the dad was on an extended call. In the melted brown sauce the boy drew loops that he accompanied with soft airplane noises.

Lucy waved to the tired young woman from the ER. The

red sweater was the right side out. Maggie brought over her cup of coffee and sat looking into it. She said, "We're back. My mom seemed okay when we got her home yesterday. She was fine."

Ilka Weiss

Ilka Weiss lay on the sofa with her legs up. She asked for a blanket. Little David helped, impatiently, to tuck it around his grandmother's legs. He said, "So, go on."

Maggie said, "Let Grandmother rest," but Ilka said, "So the next time King David went down to fight those Philistines ..." and Maggie said, "Mom, Jeff and I stay away from the fighting."

"Mommy," said little David, "you can go. And take Stevie. Stevie, stop it." Baby Steven's newest skill was turning pages and he was practicing on the King James Bible on Grandmother's lap.

"Not to worry. I know the story in my head. But let's let Mommy and Stevie stay, because we're coming to the *baaaad* stuff."

"Go *on*," the little boy said.

"King David," went on Ilka, "was a great soldier, the soldier of soldiers, only he was growing old. King David was tired. His spear was an encumbrance." Grandmother Ilka demonstrated the difficulty with which the aging king raised his weapon. "His armor was too heavy for him. Climbing the hill, he had to reach for one little low bush after another because his balance wasn't what it used to be. He watched with a thrill of envy—with a thrill and with envy—how his young soldiers ran ahead while he stood and just breathed. Couldn't tell if it was his hiatus hernia, his heart, or an attack of anxiety because they all three felt the same."

"And," little David prompted.

"And Ishbi-benob, a Philistine of the race of giants, was wearing his new armor. *His* spear weighed three hundred shekels." Grandmother lightly swung the idea of its superhuman weight above her head, "and he was going to strike King David down when—Stevie, if you don't leave King James alone, Grandmother can't check the name of the fellow—here he is in verse 17: Abishai. *He* came and struck Ishbi-benob to death."

"Mom!"

"Sorry," Ilka said. "And King David's men said to King David, 'You're becoming a liability. Next war, you're staying home.' And there was another war . . ." Ilka looked apologetically at her daughter, "and there was another giant. He had six fingers on each hand and six toes on each foot—which is how many digits, quick!"

"Twenty-four."

"Very good. And this giant with his twenty-four digits just laughed at King David, and mocked him."

"Why?" asked little David in a tone of strong disapproval.

"Why? Why indeed!" said his grandmother. "Because King David was old? Because he was a Hebrew? Just because he was on the other team? But King David's nephew—*his* name was Jonathan—came running, and Jonathan knocked that mocking, laughing giant down just a little bit. Knocked the wind out of him."

Little David suggested, "They should have tried talking it out," in which he was going to remember being reinforced by a hug from his mother, and his grandmother's kiss on the top of his head, for both women were against striking people dead, and the younger believed there was something one could be doing about it.

"They should have talked," Grandmother Ilka agreed, "without precondition. And now," she went on, "King David got really, *really* old and stricken in years and they brought him a blanket and another and more blankets but he could not and could not get warm."

"How come?" asked little David.

"Because he was old," Grandmother Ilka said. "And King David's men said to him, "Let us go out and find you a beautiful young girl to lie with you."

"What for?" asked little David.

"To make him warm. The blankets hadn't done any good. So they sent out throughout all the land and found a beautiful young girl. Her name was Abishag the Shunammite and they brought her to the king."

"Did she want to come?" asked David.

"A very troubling question," said his grandmother.

"I always thought it was horrible," said his mother.

"Yes, it was! Well, hold on, now. You know," she said to David, "how your mommy had to rush me to Emergency, and then I was in the hospital, and had to go for rehab, and your mommy brought me back, and last night I had to go to Emergency again, and your daddy is coming in half an hour to take you and Stevie home, and Mommy is going to stay and take care of me? Maybe Abishag was one of those people who stay and take care of people, like your mommy, because she is good, which is a great mystery to the rest of us."

"Mom, don't," said Maggie irritably. "I do it because I want to."

"Which," said Ilka, continuing to address the child, "is another mystery: Good people *don't* think they are being good when they *like* doing a good thing. If they did it with gritted teeth, then they would think that it was good! Isn't that funny of them?"

The little boy was listening to the old woman with an alert, bemused look.

"And Abishag," continued his grandmother, "was young and beautiful and she cared for King David."

"And made him warm."

"No."

"By three in the morning we had to call the ambulance," Maggie told Lucy. "They say they've found her a bed in Observation and my mom's turfed me out. She wants me to go home."

"That's right! I told my son to go home," Lucy said.

"A hot bath!" the young woman said. "A couple of hours' sleep if my husband can drop my little boy off at school and take the baby to the sitter ..."

"Of course he can!" said Lucy. "And you'll come back at visiting hours tomorrow."

"That's what I'm going to do," the young woman said, but she went on sitting.

Lucy was about to tell her about Maurie not calling, and not accepting, not rejecting "Rumpelstiltskin," but the young woman took out her cell. She put through a call to the visiting nurse to tell her not to come, and one to the baby's sitter to change her hours. She tried in vain to get through to Kastel Street and was unable to reach her husband to give him the address of David's after-school playdate, and she tried Kastel Street again. "I'll call them from home."

Lucy wished her good luck.

The stout black dad and his too-well-behaved boy had left.

The couple, the man and the woman, were done eating. They rose. He stood while she bused the tray. Lucy said to him, "Excuse me, do you know what day this is?"

The man, like the teenage brother in the ER, drew his head backward. He frowned. "What?"

Lucy said, "I'm supposed to meet some people and I'm wondering if this is the wrong day?"

"Tuesday," said the man and turned in the direction from which he was relieved to see his wife returning. Lucy watched them, he two steps ahead of her, walking together, toward the exit.

The blond couple were talking to their BlackBerrys. And Lucy remembered her cell phone. She opened her handbag and there it was; here were her reading glasses. Here was her address book. She found and she dialed Freddy Wells's number.

"This is Lucy!"

Dear Freddy! She could tell that he was pleased. "Lucy! A long time! That's New York for you!" Freddy said he was well—well, he was well enough. Lisa was well enough. How was Lucy?

"Pretty well. Can you imagine my son Benedict and I are colleagues in the same office?" The first items of information, which old acquaintances who have not talked in a while exchange with each other, tend to be the kind that are of no interest to the other or indeed to anyone. Lucy knew that Freddy would just as soon not hear the dates and details of Maurie's neither accepting, rejecting, nor so much as acknowledging receipt of a story she had originally called "Emergency!" and changed to "Ambulance," changed to "Nine One One." "Till I realized," Lucy told Freddy, "that it spells 'Nine Eleven,' which isn't what this story is about. It is—and of course isn't—about Bertie's last illness. I call it 'Rumpelstiltskin in Emergency,' a short-short. I can read it to you," Lucy said, and she started reading.

" '*Don't don't don't call the doctor!*' " read Lucy. " '*What does the doctor know?' murmurs the man who is in pain. He tosses himself onto his side, his other side. 'Call the doctor!' shrieks his whisper. 'NOW!*' "

Freddy said, "Lucy, I want to hear your story, but Lisa is—Lisa is about to get dinner on the table."

Lucy's capacity for observation did not depend on her five senses. She was able to envisage the clever Lisa Wells—a bit of a pill but Lucy rather liked her—drawing a question mark in the air of her Philadelphia living room where Lucy had been an occasional dinner guest. Lucy imagined Freddy shrugging and, using the hand not holding the telephone, making the motion that signifies, What the hell do you want me to do?

Lucy said, "It's a short-short, a few pages," and continued reading:

"*A three-count. The driver and the ambulance attendant shunt the man in pain onto the stretcher. From inside the ambulance, its wail is muted and can be ignored. The man in pain pushes and pulls at the restraints that hold him down on his back when he needs to turn onto his side. He needs to sit up and double over.*"

Fred's voice in Lucy's ear said, "Lisa reminds me we have people coming—people are coming over."

"*The ambulance attendant is young and tall. 'Where do you experience the pain?' he asks the patient, who is trying to locate the sensation that tells him he is going to throw up again.*"

Fred Wells said, "Lucy, this is harrowing and deserves a better hearing than I can give it with these people coming right over," and indeed, Lucy could hear them—the people, in Philadelphia, ringing the Wells' front-door bell, unless Lisa had slipped out and was ringing it. Freddy said, "If Maurie doesn't publish, send it to me at *The Reader*."

"Nope. Never no more no more no more!" said Lucy. "Sending your work out is like sending your kid to school when you won't know if he ever even arrived! '*The ambulance attendant asks the patient how long he has had this pain, another question to which he does not have the answer: "Hours! Hours and hours, months, off and on for maybe a year,"*' " read Lucy into a silence like no other—the empty line of a phone that has been hung up.

At a point in the afternoon, Benedict ran up to his mother's apartment from where he called Al: "She's picked up her mail."

"Who?" said Al.

"My mom. I called at noon and she was on her landline. She must just have gone out again. When I call her on her cell, it's engaged! I know she's not going to return my messages, because she wouldn't let me show her how to do voice mail."

Al said, "When my dad got my nana her first dishwasher she soaped every dish before she put it in the machine—knew she didn't have to, said it made her guilty, but she couldn't help herself."

Benedict felt lonely. Al was a good kid but he couldn't join Benedict in his growing anxiety about Lucy. Benedict called Gretel but her cell was off. He tried Lucy again. Who would she be talking to and where was she?

Benedict was on his way home when he decided to go

back to Cedars, where he bungled into a lecture in progress. The students wore nurses' uniforms. The lecturer was a gray-haired nurse. She pointed to a diagram on a computer screen. "You will be expected to be able to review, one, the prevalence and variety of types of dementia; two, the interrelationship between the various types of dementia and medical comorbidities; three, the role of depression as a prodrome, risk factor, and manifestation of dementia; four ..." Benedict backed out and closed the door, and the student in the last row, who had turned to see who was coming in, turned back to peek at her neighbor's notes and copy what she had missed.

Salman Haddad's secretary wanted to know how *she* was expected to know the whereabouts of Benedict's mother. Mr. Haddad, she imagined, had gone home after he and Mr. Bernstine went over to check out the seventh floor.

"Which seventh floor is this?"

"The *seventh floor*! In the *Senior Center*!" as any fool would know, implied Haddad's assistant's tone, "that they're turning into a holding area for the sixty-two-pluses from the ER." No sense his going over there till they opened it in the morning, and the assistant tossed things into her handbag, making it plain that wherever other people might or might not be going, *she* was going to go home.

Benedict, too, went home, annoyed that it bothered him to have gotten on some snarky secretary's nerves. He was unreasonably irritated to find Gretel's message that she was going to be late after *his* long day's low-grade panic about Lucy. Gretel's cell was still off, his mother's was still busy, and Benedict found himself ambushed by his own rage. If Joe had committed Lucy to another night of "observation" on this seventh floor that nobody had told anybody anything about ... And *what* was Joe's Wide-Open Eye bunch doing in the service of Cedars of Lebanon, anyway? Lebanon! Who were these Haddads and what was wrong with them that they had chosen Joe and his computer whiz kids and an elderly poet with emphysema to investigate—WHAT?

Benedict left messages for Joe, one on his cell and one on his landline: "Where are you? What the hell have you done with my mother?"

Lucy's address book fell open at the S's. Snodgrass, De, dead a year and more. Lucy read "Rumpelstiltskin" to Barry S., an old student of Lucy's who had acute, smart, and friendly things to say about her story. So did Matt, another old student, terrific writer.

Lucy turned back, and starting properly with the A's, went alphabetically down the list of her friends, acquaintances, and the people one knew from a long life in the writing world—some famous, the near-famous, the midlist, the still-unknowns, those who were going to remain unknown. She called Jeffery. He was not home. Lucy suspected presences barricaded behind every outgoing message. The D's. Sally had died in 2008. John G. had been dead these twenty years. Lucy hadn't the heart to remove their addresses.

If someone was home and picked up, she said "Hi! This is Lucy," and whether they said, "Lucy! For goodness' sake! Telepathy! You won't believe that I was this minute thinking of calling you!" or "Lucy! Good to hear your voice! Can I call you back? I had one foot out the door," or, "We are just sitting down to dinner!" or "Lucy, my *dear*! I'm in the middle of this silly thing I've been following on the TV," Lucy said, "This'll take all of three minutes, a short-short. I call it 'Rumpelstiltskin in Emergency,'" and would start reading. Alan on the West Coast said he'd taken early retirement from teaching creative writing so he would never again have to correct syntactic infelicities, two of which he pointed out in Lucy's short-short, and he was right. He was good. Tom, Stanley, and Victoria respectively liked, really loved, thought it was the best thing she had ever done. Norman said it was interesting, and then he read Lucy a story of his called "The Pepper Tree" which, he said, had him tied in knots. Vivian said, "*You* know that this is not my cup of tea," and Jeffery was still out. Sophie called Jordan to pick up the extension and they listened to Lucy read her story.

" *'Is the pain constant or only when you move?' the ambulance attendant asks the man whose pain has become a component of his person while, with certain, sudden movements, it knocks a sound out of him between a yelp and a cough. 'Both,' he answers. The ambulance attendant is new at the job. He suspends his pen over the report, which he will hand in when they arrive at the hospital. He is supposed to check either 'constant'* or *'when you move.' Next question: 'Would you call this a dull or a stabbing pain?' 'Dull! Hell hell hell! No, I would not call this pain a dull pain! God. And I would not call it "stabbing."' The man in pain focuses* on *the pain, the exact location of which, and its origin in time, he is unable to pinpoint: He compares what he feels with what he understands the word 'stabbing' to connote and stabbing is not what this is, nor is it 'biting,' 'shooting,' 'burning,' 'searing,' 'throbbing,' 'grinding,' or 'gnawing.' He searches the language and does not find in its vocabulary the word that names this peculiar excruciation. 'Get me* Roget's Thesaurus*!' shrieks the man in pain."*

Over the top of the page that she was reading, Lucy could see the undersized waitress walking toward her. Where was the blond couple and their BlackBerrys? Lucy had not seen them go, nor had she noticed the staff upturning chairs onto the tables; one pulled the head of an enormous mop between two rollers that squeezed an overload of water into a bucket the size of a young bathtub. Lucy recognized the bite, inside her nostrils, of industrial-strength disinfectant. Lucy read:

"The ambulance has come to a stop below the overhang outside Emergency. The ambulance attendant folds the report into an outside pocket of the black bag that he slings over his shoulder. He jumps out and walks around the ambulance to open the back door. 'Wants a Roget's Thesaurus,*' the ambulance attendant says to the uniformed attendant who has come to assist him. They have to readjust the straps, which the patient's writhings have loosened, before they pull the stretcher out and snap it onto its wheels on the tarmac. 'Wants a what?' The uniformed attendant receives the patient's report from the ambulance attendant in exchange*

for the address of the next patient to be picked up. The ambulance attendant hops back into the ambulance."

Lucy knew that the waitress was standing to talk to her. "Miss, the cafeteria is closing."

"One more page!" Lucy promised the waitress, who continued to stand another moment before she walked away.

" *'One two three.' They shunt him over onto a gurney that the uniformed attendant wheels through the self-opening doors into Emergency.* 'Roget's Thesaurus!' *moans the man in pain to a passing nurse whose shift is over; she is on her way home.*"

The waitress returned with the manager. "The cafeteria is closed, miss," the manager told Lucy, who held up a hand. While the manager phoned down to Emergency saying, "Got one in the cafeteria. Around the bend, looks like. You better send a chair," Lucy finished the story:

"*The Emergency doctor asks the patient how long he has been experiencing the pain. 'What do you mean, you don't know? When did you first have this pain? A week, two weeks ago? You don't know! Where do you feel it? You don't know where you feel the pain?' The doctor palpates the patient, who screams. The doctor knows where the pain is! This doctor is old and bald. He looks like a doctor. The man in pain asks him, 'What is wrong with me?' The doctor says, 'We'll know more when we've done a couple of tests.' There are many patients in Emergency and the doctor has to get this one to release the sleeve of his white coat. 'What' cries the patient, 'is its name?' 'Rumpelstiltskin!' the doctor says. The man in pain is throwing up again.*"

Patrice was the orderly with the powerfully developed upper arms. He had placed fourth in last year's NABBA USA Bodybuilding Conference and applied his educated force to maneuvering the old woman's legs out from under the table. She gave him zero help. While he lifted the patient into the wheelchair and wheeled her, with her PATIENTS PROPERTY bag balanced on her lap, to Emergency, she was turning the page of her address book.

Lucy was, mercifully, not going to call her friend Katherine who had spent a lifetime persuading friends, acquaintances, and all the people she knew to let her be the lone writer, the writer in the attic. Who was Lucy to argue that a good novel isn't better than the best friendship, and Katherine's novels were good on the grand scale.

Emergency would not receive Lucy Friedgold. The ER was in the process of transferring its demented sixty-two-pluses to the new holding area. There were the necessary phone calls and the multiplying paperwork. Patrice had learned to make use of these downtimes, the frequent long waits associated with his job in the Cedars of Lebanon's ER. He practiced pumping iron intellectually. Patrice had time to visualize the choreography of his routine from the first to the final freeze in detail, editing his mistakes before Nurse Trotwood handed him Lucy's Intake Form for Seniors to take along to the Senior Center's seventh floor.

Lucy found James under the M's and read him

"Rumpelstiltskin in Emergency" while Patrice wheeled her up the sidewalk and through the great doors. James said it was good.

Jack and Hope

Some days after the lunch at the Café Provence, Jeremy had to take his father to Cedars of Lebanon's Emergency. He called Nora and Nora called her mother.

"Jack's in the hospital. They were going to send him home but he started to cry. Mom?"

"Yes," said her mother.

"They've moved him to the Senior Center. Mom! Are you there?"

"Yes," said Hope.

"Do you want me to take you over?"

"Yes."

Nora came to pick her mother up. "You want me to pin up your hair for you?"

"No. This is my Arbus persona."

"Your which? Mom, what are you talking *about*?"

The Sabbath Elevator opens and closes its door on every floor without having its buttons pressed. Hope stepped in behind an orderly who was pushing a wheelchair. "Miss," the orderly was saying, "it's not going to work in here," but the old woman in the chair continued to poke the buttons on her cell phone and hold it to her ear. Hope looked around her at a congregation of gargoyles: The huge old black woman might have been poured to overflowing into her wheelchair; her mouth stood open as if there were no room inside for the restless lolling of her purple tongue. The freakishly long, thin, banged-up old Don Quixote wore an anachronistic smile and so did the little stick-figure manikin next to him, and next to *him*, her waist bent at a ninety-degree angle, was the prototype of Hansel and Gretel's witch, whose crooked nose met with her stubbled chin. And when Hope turned to Nora's loved face, she saw it rammed down to the left into the shape of an earlier phase of the human type: Nora was watching an old peasant that we don't see on the New York streets, who was unbuttoning the front of her dress. She reached her navel as the Sabbath Elevator opened its doors to discharge its cargo on the Senior Center's seventh floor.

IV
The Seventh Floor

The seventh floor has been temporarily designated an annex to the ER, to hold the demented sixty-two-pluses. The Senior Center is the most recent addition, and the northmost building of the hospital complex, which covers several city blocks between the two avenues. The Center's architect had interned with the Lincoln Square Renewal Project under Robert Moses, and had built his glass-and-iron structure to incorporate the movements of the hospital's population of patients, staff, and doctors as an integral idea of design.

Lucy sits in the solarium facing the glass wall backed by blackest night and observes her reflected self in the wheelchair. The YTREPORP STNEITAP bag is on her lap, the cell phone at her ear. "Stephen!" she says, "This is Lucy! A voice out of your past …"

"Mom?"

"Benedict? How come? I dialed Stephen."

"Mom, where the hell are you? What is going on?"

"Dear, I can't talk now. I'm reading Stephen 'Rumpelstiltskin in Emergency.' "

"Mom, why didn't you wait for Joe in the waiting room like I told you?"

"I went to the cafeteria. Do you know they've completely redone the whole thing? I bagged a table for the meeting only nobody showed up. What time did you say the meeting was scheduled for?"

"It wasn't. I didn't say. We were waiting for Joe to get out of the ER. Mom, where *is* Joe?"

"He's right here. We came up in the elevator together. Ben, look, I can't talk …"

"Mom, I told you Joe wanted to debrief you. Why are you still at Cedars?"

"Ben, I'm on the phone reading a story to Stephen and I can't talk."

"Mom, is it your emphysema?"

Lucy has hung up.

Hope and Nora have found Room 702, where Jack sits in his wheelchair and weeps. Hope, in her day, had wept—wept for Jack—but she had covered her mouth or hidden her face in her hands. Jack weeps with his neck outstretched, exposing his throat. His chin points at the ceiling or what is missing beyond. He is in physical despair, and weeps and is too spent to remember how to stop.

Ida and the Crazy Box

The hospital reaches Marta, Ida Farkasz's daughter, in her store and asks her to pick up her mother from the seventh floor of the Senior Center and take her home. Marta checks the time on the clock but does not take the time to check her prematurely graying hair in the mirror. Ida notices and says, "You wouldn't go to a customer looking like that, but for mother this is okay?"

"Mama, I left the store in the middle of a working day, and I'm here."

"Next time, I'll know to put myself into the hospital, instead of sitting in my apartment that doesn't even have a window so I could see what's going on out in the street, waiting for it to occur to you to come and see me."

Marta says, "Mama, I come to see you."

"And get on your phone," Ida says, "and start calling your friends, which is just as well because the only way I find out what's going on in your life is overhearing you telling other people."

"The person I just called was my assistant, and what's going on is my not getting three dozen deliveries boxed and to the post office, which I'll be having to do tomorrow, which is already over-scheduled."

"While I sit on a chair in my apartment waiting for you to call me, and have maybe a conversation?"

"The only conversation you and I have is about my not calling and my not visiting. Mama, why don't I phone Poldi? She's not well, and she wants to see you." Marta laughs and says, "Mama, you're looking into the crazy box ..."

"Looking into the crazy box," "*Ins Narrenkastl schauen*," was what Ida said *her* mother used to call it when the thing in front of your eyes is blotted out by a more powerful inner vision. Ida stares at the shoe she holds in her hands and is not putting on her foot. What she sees in the crazy box is herself and Poldi passing Miss Margate's building and Poldi stepping up the first step to block the entrance with her body.

"Call Poldi," spits Ida. "Tell her if she comes I'll throw her out on her ear."

"Okay, Mama. Where did they put your jacket? Did you have a jacket?"

The photo album, which has migrated from Pressburg to the Dominican Republic to New York, lies open on the table when Marta comes out of the bedroom where she has put away her mother's clothes.

Ida says, "Your father, with his little Hitler mustache."

"Mama, I've got to go. I'm sorry."

"Summer 1935, before they closed the swim baths. *Juden ist der Eintritt Verboten*. We used to go every Sunday and stay all day. Lining up to jump in the pool, look at Kari always clowning. Poldi, best figure of anybody, but it was Berta who had the loveliest face. Here's your father, a little man. Onkel Igo. Maxl, Terry. You see where I've put their names on the back. When I'm gone who will remember who they ever were?"

"Mama, I have to go and close up the store."

"Go, close. Go and close up. Go go go go."

Deb and Shirley

Dr. Miriam Haddad has walked over to the Senior Center. She looks into Samson Gorewitz's room, sees the two sisters sitting with their brother, and backs away. She takes her time in the nurse's station, reviewing the information. Glenshore has transcribed the material from Samson's wet wallet: the Columbus, Ohio, address, and his life in numbers: SSN; born 03/08/28; phone numbers; phone number of the sister residing in New York. The doctor looks over the Intake Form: Education, OSU; Nearest Relative, a son (?) in pairs (!); Occupation, ran (?) a "peppermill" (?!). Next to Comments the intern has written: One-sided facial paralysis (?) makes patient's speech difficult/impossible to follow. May be confused/demented (??).

Shirley is reading Deborah an article titled "Which City Hospital Is Driving Seniors Insane?"

"Is this a joke?"

Shirley says, "Listen."

" '*Our source, whose identity we vow to face incarceration to protect, reports that elderly patients checking into the emergency room of one of our city's major teaching facilities check out with what the hospital's spokesperson, Dr. Miriam Haddad, . . .'* "

"Our Arab!" Deb and Shirley look hilariously at each other.

"She's Jewish," Samson says.

" '*. . . what the hospital's spokesperson, Dr. Miriam Haddad, for lack of a diagnosis, is calling "copycat Alzheimer's."*' "

"It's a joke!" Deb says.

" '*There is no emergency room,' states Dr. Haddad, 'that is not liable to raise the stress level to one that can cause temporary dementia, particularly in the elderly.' When pressed to estimate the incidence of cases of dementia in percentages, she put it at a cool 100.*"

The sisters look over at Sammy, who lies on the bed and looks at the ceiling. His hands are folded on his stomach. His burbling speech—is it the monologue of dementia?

" '*The hospital's security officer, Salman Haddad . . .*' "

"Another one!" Deb says.

"*. . . has retained Joseph Bernstine, former CEO of the Concordance Institute, to check into this curious statistic. We reached Mr. Bernstine in the hospital's Senior Center, where he is himself, at the time of this writing, a patient. Mr. Bernstine suggested the possibility of a terrorist connection.*"

"It's a put-on!"

" ' "*We know,*" *says Bernstine,* "*that an operative with a cell phone in Dublin, or in Dubai, can cause a bomb to detonate in Times Square just as easily as in the Old City of Jerusalem. We are beginning to look into the possibility of long-distance cyber-manipulations inside enclosed areas such as emergency facilities."' "*

"Shirley, this is a joke!"

"Like 9/11 was a joke?"

"More like a Washington plot," says Deb. "You don't think it's curious that the hospital's security officer and the ER's spokesperson are Haddads?"

Sam says it again: "She's Jewish."

"Okay, sweetheart. It's okay," they say to him. "By the way," Deb asks Shirley, "what was he doing in Glenshore in the first place?"

"It's where we spent that summer—Uncle Seymour came down, don't you remember?" says Deb.

"Another summer we didn't get to go to Israel, is what I remember," says Shirley, and Samson, his right hand in Shirley's, his left in Deb's hand, watches them slide inevitably down, like two people rolling into the depression of an old mattress, into their lifelong argument.

Discussion had been constant in the Gorewitz home. Uncle Seymour might draw out of his pocket an article from the *Forward* with which their father agreed, or radically disagreed, and could have backed, alternatively challenged with a quotation, if someone had not moved the book—it was the fat one with the green spine, which should have been on this shelf right here, or here; he had to quote the relevant passage from memory. No one waited or was expected to wait for anyone to finish speaking. If an opposing argument wanted to make itself heard, it raised its volume. The three Gorewitz children had breathed in secondary opinion. If either of the two clever little girls voiced one of her own, the grown-ups beamed.

When Uncle Seymour asked Samson what he was going to grow up to be, the little boy said, "A stand-up comic," and his sisters' groans, their calling on the Lord's name in vain, could not stop him from performing his favorite old rabbi joke: Dave comes to the rabbi to argue that a certain field is his field. The rabbi listens and says, "You're right. That field is yours." On his way out, Dave passes Sid. Sid is coming to the rabbi to argue that this same field is his, and the rabbi listens and says, "You're right. That is your field." Sid goes home. The rebbetzin has been listening in the next room and comes in and says, "The same field can't belong both to Dave and to Sid," and the rabbi says, "And you're right, too. It can't."

There came a season in which Samson seemed to hear the sound of escaping air, as when the human bottom came to rest on the backless leather seat in their hallway—"the pouf," his mother called it. Sam imagined two opposing poufs on which his two sisters eventually settled, Shirley on one, on the other Deborah. The relief of knowing which truth was true; which of two histories you were choosing to imagine; whose calamities were calamities and whose the eggs you had to break to make the omelet; what, once and for all, you were for, whose side you were on, who was the enemy! Neither Deborah nor Shirley ever, in the subsequent half-century, budged from their certainties. From here on in, Deborah believed and argued that everything *we* do is wrong, and what *they* do is right, or wrong only in response to the wrong we have done to them. Shirley argued that everything we did was right and anything they did, whatever the reason, was wrong. Each defended her argument with an arsenal of her own facts.

Samson's function, as he saw it, had been to irritate both by always taking an opposite position.

Samson, the Drowned Man

Dr. Haddad sees the sisters come out of the room and watches them walk in the direction of the Sabbath Elevator, and now she goes into Samson Gorewitz's room. The patient has his way of lying very still and flat on his back. His eyes are open.

The doctor cranks up the bed. "We need you to be sitting up, Mr. Gorewitz, and to sit in a chair. You have to start moving if you want to get well."

The patient says, "That's past praying for," and makes a sound like laughing.

"Now why do you say that, Mr. Gorewitz?"

The patient does not reply.

"How does one run a peppermill, Mr. Gorewitz?"

"*Paper! Paper mill.* We made the grocery cardboard boxes the color of the Judean desert, stack them, line them up, I always thought they were beautiful. Nobody stops to think that there was a person who engineered the way they fold flat for storage, how cleverly they reassemble."

"Mr. Gorewitz, you know where you are?"

"I told that boy, in heaven."

"You are in heaven, Mr. Gorewitz?"

" 'If they find me not, look in the other place.' Jews don't worry about it so much. You're Jewish."

"Of course," says Dr. Haddad. "Are you dead, Mr. Gorewitz?"

"Drowned on Glenshore beach. If you're Jewish, why do you wear the what-do-you-call-it over your hair, if you don't mind my asking?"

"The hijab," Dr. Miriam says with some little irritation. "Why does that spook people? My bubbe covered her head with a beautifully coiffured shaitel. She was a doctor before her time, and a dresser. My favorite Aunt Bernice teaches philosophy. I don't know that she even knows she wears her own hair disguised as a shaitel with a fringe across her forehead, and a hair clip. What is this *thing* we have with our hair? Some women cover it, and the men? These ones put hats on when they enter the house of their god; that lot takes their hats off. The hat!" said Dr. Miriam Haddad, and was quiet for a moment. "On my Sunday walks with Grandpa Abner," she said, "his hat used to measure the importance of the people we passed, especially the ladies. Grandpa would touch his hand to the brim, or grasp the brim between thumb and forefinger to just suggest lifting it; there was the little lift, and there was the grand sweep. And my uncle Shimon—my little sister and I used to imagine him in bed with his yarmulke on. So I wear the hijab like my mother- and sisters-in-law. My husband likes it."

"Isn't it confining?"

"So's my white doctor's coat. So are your pants. Nothing is tighter on you than your skin. What makes you think you're dead, Mr. Gorewitz? Your medical report says you're alive. We're surprised—we're rather puzzled in fact, by your recovery."

"Dead or alive," Samson says, "where's the difference? Who knew there would be a ceiling in heaven, and a floor, windows, a bed, the TV, and Deb and Shirley arguing through eternity?"

"So, Mr. Gorewitz, if everything is the same, why do you think that you are dead?"

"Ah, that old trick! That won't work," Samson says. "Pinch yourself. If you don't feel it, you're asleep; if it hurts you must be awake? What if you pinch yourself and you're dead and it hurts the same as it does when you're alive; that," says Samson in a tone of ultimate clarity, "is the gyp."

"What is a gyp, Mr. Gorewitz?"

"Being dead."

On her way to the Sabbath Elevator, Dr. Haddad passes the open door of Room 711 and stops, surprised to see the Gorewitz sisters sitting on the edges of the two beds. Their profiled faces are opposed to each other, the mouths of both are in motion.

Deborah and Shirley are engaged in the conversation that resembles a never-ending pas de deux in which Deborah foreknows the move Shirley will make in response to the last move, that she, Deborah, has made, knowing the response that she will make to Shirley's response to it. Each believes that the next thing she is going to say will so newformulate the self-evident truth that it must expose the other's mistaken assumptions and make an end of the dance once and for all.

Dr. Haddad returns to the nurses' station. She asks the nurse, "What's with the two women in seven-eleven?"

"Around the bend," the nurse answers.

Muzac of the Sheres

Francis Rhinelander is one of the gargoyles whom Hope observed coming up in the Sabbath Elevator. The young doctor with the good head of hair had taken care of his facial cuts and abrasions and sent him to the Release Office two doors to the right of the triage window to sign himself out, but here he is back again. Phyllis has sent Al Lesser over to follow up on his earlier interview. Al sees that something has happened. There is a difference in the sag of the tall old man's shoulders, in his ruined smile. He sits on the edge of his bed and ducks his head. With his chin he indicates the wall-mounted TV on which a beautiful specimen of young manhood is selling a new technology not obtainable in stores or through the mails, for only four easy value-pays of $19.95 plus shipping and handling.

The old man shakes and shakes his head.

"Just some old infomercial," Al says to him.

"I know, but *listen*," Rhinelander says.

Al and his patient watch the specimen demonstrate the Twice-Told®, a plastic headband with a built-in nano computer that translates the movements of eye and facial musculature of the person sitting across from you and tells you "You've told this story to this person before," *before* you have started telling it once again.

"Where do you have your remote? You can just turn it off," Al suggests.

"*Listen!*"

The specimen guarantees us our money back, no questions asked, if we are not completely satisfied.

"The music," the old man says, "while the man is talking."

It is now that Al Lesser hears what is too familiar to notice, the ongoing, anonymous, circular thrumming.

"*Why?*" Rhinelander says in his despair.

"Oh, well, because, I mean," Al says, "you have to have music."

"*Do* you?"

"It would be—wouldn't it be, I don't know—kind of bald without some music?"

"Would it?" The sad old man ducks. He nods his head. "My waiter can turn Frank Sinatra down but never *off.* Frank Sinatra doesn't *turn* off, not even *in the john*, and I can't go with Sinatra in the john singing 'The Way You Look Tonight'! Frank Sinatra in my cereal. I walked to Gristedes at the corner, going to get myself something and eat it up in my hotel room, but Frank Sinatra was signing 'My Way' in the bread aisle and in the dairy aisle and when I got back to my room, he was singing 'New York, New York.' I called maintenance. It seems they won't remove the TV out of the room but they said they could disconnect it, but then he got on my little plastic radio I have on the seat of the chair next to my bed. I pushed the Off button so hard I pushed it all the way in. I can hear it rattling around on the inside. I can't get it out, so I went down and got in a cab to come back here. They have TV in all the cabs. The 'off' button turns the music *ON.*"

Francis Rhinelander and Al Lesser sit and watch the specimen. He is on a high of enthusiasm, saying, "But wait!" and guarantees *two* Twice-Tolds® to everyone who calls within the next three minutes while the circling thrumming prevents the baldness of silence.

Francis Rhinelander says, "The reason the management never answered my letter is there *is* no Off option! No one can turn off the Muzak of the Spheres." His head ducks up and down and up and down like a toy set in motion by a child's finger.

The Ice Worm

The mistake was to have taken the advice of the woman in the cafeteria and gone home and left her mother in the ER. It is morning. Maggie goes straight to Observation, where they know nothing of any Ilka Weiss. "The doctor said you had a bed for her."

"What doctor?"

"The doctor in the ER."

"Better go down there, then."

It's a leisurely morning in the waiting area. A young mom closes the picture book she has been trying to read to her toddler. The boy, around Stevie's age, prefers climbing over the benches.

A neat, dapper little man is talking with the nurse through the triage window. Maggie stands waiting behind him. She assumes he is an official person, and that this may be an official conversation. A harried young man comes and stands behind Maggie; she experiences his impatience uncomfortably. The probably official person folds his arms on the sill of the triage window so that now his head is inside the office; this is going to take time. Maggie leaves her place in line and walks to the door that leads into the ER and knocks on it. When nobody answers, she opens it to face a large, surprised nurse. This is not a nurse Maggie recognizes from last night. The nurse looks put-upon: *No*, Maggie can*not* come in to see if her mother is inside. There is no Ilka

Weiss in the ER. *Yes*, the nurse is certain, and she does *not* know where Ilka Weiss might have been transferred during the night. Who might know? Triage might know, or go to the Release Office. She points to a door on the left.

Maggie sees that she has lost her place behind the official person, and behind the harried young man stands an old woman holding her older husband by the arm.

A uniformed guard leans in the doorway of the Release Office. The officer sits at his desk saying, "Is that right!" and "Is that a fact!"

"Over there and large as life!" the guard says. "This old broad takes off every last stitch."

"You don't say."

"Stands buck naked."

Speaking over the guard's shoulder, Maggie says, "Excuse me, but would you know where they transferred my mother? The name is Ilka Weiss? I left because they told me they had a bed for her in Observation, but they don't have her in Observation."

Nobody, it turns out, has left the ER since the Release Officer came on at 8:30. According to the roster there have been no releases after midnight.

"So she must still be in the ER?" Maggie says.

"Could might have eloped." The guard grins.

Unfortunately, it is the put-upon nurse at the door again. She says, "Are you going to argue with me? We do *not* have Ilka Weiss in this ER."

Dr. Haddad, the doctor on night duty, has left. It happens to be her day off, and the doctor who takes Maggie's call is not acquainted with the situation. The nurse wears the look that comes into the eyes of official persons at a first suspicion that they're dealing with someone who is going to be trouble: a kook. *No*, Maggie cannot go into the ER and check for herself. "*I* will check *for* you," says the nurse, who does not care *who* knows that put-upon is what she is.

It's almost noon before Maggie gets hold of her husband. "They've gone and lost my mom! That nurse didn't take long enough to have checked every gurney and looked behind all the curtains in all the cubicles! I think they've got her disguised with bandages like what's-her-name in what was the name of that Hitchcock movie?" Joking fails to override a small ice worm of panic that has started in Maggie's chest.

"Call information," Jeff says.

"I did. And I went down where you enter and talked to the woman who gives out the visitor passes, and they have no record of my mom ever even checking *in*!"

"Let me try calling information from outside."

There are moments when Maggie loves her husband: He is doing this *with her*. "Jeff, thanks, Jeff. Jeff, call me right back!" The worm has attached itself in the middle of Maggie's chest, where the ribs meet. Whom doth time stand still withal? Somebody waiting for somebody to call right back. Maggie cannot wait another nanosecond and calls Jeff, whose line is busy, of course, trying, maybe, to call her? Hang up, and wait for him to call. Maggie starts at Jeff's voice in her ear:

"The reason they've got no record of Ilka's admission is she came in via Emergency. Why don't you go down there?"

"That is where I am. Jeff, I'm *in* the waiting area. There must be some reason why they won't let me into the ER to see for myself..."

"Maggie," Jeff says, "love, remember your monster scenarios when I'm late, or David isn't where you imagine he's supposed to be? The explanation that doesn't occur to you turns out to be mind-numbingly obvious?"

"I know. Right. You're right. I will remember. There's somebody coming to talk to me? I'll talk to you later."

It's the dapper man—Arab? Indian?—who was talking with triage. "If your mother was in the ER, she's been transferred to the seventh floor in the Senior Center."

Maggie needs to keep the worm from wriggling upward and spreading its mortal chill. She asks, "The Senior Center? Doesn't that mean they didn't find anything really wrong with her?"

"Nothing physically, necessarily. Old people's confusions are often temporary." Maggie scans his face for a gloss, an annotation. He says, "Nurse, tell the lady the best way to get over to the Senior Center."

Patrice had pushed Lucy's wheelchair the two blocks up the sidewalk, but the Senior Center can also be reached by taking the elevator down to the connecting sub-sub-basements.

Because Maggie has chosen this option, Jeff's call cannot reach her. She doesn't know that the hospital has phoned to say that Ilka is agitated and calling for Maggie, asking who is going to pay for what she seems to think is a room in a hotel. Jeff says, "I'll bring the boys over and see if they'll let Ilka see them."

Maggie feels herself to be hiking for a period outside ordinary time, through an unsuspected, unpeopled underground of white, brightly lighted corridors. The unmarked doors must open from within, for there are no visible handles or knobs. Maggie walks and keeps walking in a spatial equivalent of eternity where what is ahead is in no particular distinguishable from where she has been. Maggie pushes through a series of swinging doors into new reaches of corridors like the ones along which she is walking. She glances down corridors that branch to the left and right. Why does she think it is the one she is continuing to move along that will take her to her destination, that will have an end? To turn and retrace her steps occurs to her, but do we stop and put our nightmares in reverse? Maggie pushes viciously through the next set of doors into a corridor that squares into a room and has a bank of perfectly ordinary elevators.

Maggie steps out into the sunny, modern seventh floor with its ample space around the central nurses' station. Here, having arrived before her, is the impatient young man from the waiting area, who turns out to be looking for *his* mother. "Is it her emphysema acting up?" he asks the nurse. Benedict waits for the nurse's eyes to detach from the computer screen to which he is acutely aware of not having access. He looks behind him and sees, spread-eagled on a recliner, the square old woman, the one who took off her clothes in the waiting area last night, and she is mother-naked. Like drunken Noah's two good sons, Shem and Japheth, Benedict turns his back to the forbidden nakedness while like Ham, the wicked son, he turns his head to cop another look.

"Excuse me," he says to the Computer Nurse, "that woman has taken off her gown."

The nurse says, "You're looking for who?"

"My mother, Lucy Friedgold? Is it her emphysema?"

"Friedgold," says the nurse. "Came in last night. Does not have emphysema."

"F-R-I-E-D-gold. Lucy. My mother?"

"No emphysema."

"Can I have a look at that?" says Benedict.

"No, you cannot," says the nurse. "She's in Room seven-twelve."

"And do you have a Joe Bernstine?"

"Room seven-oh-six."

"Maggie!"

Maggie hears her mother calling and there she is, Ilka sitting in a chair in a fresh hospital gown.

"Here you are!" Maggie kisses her. "Major mix-up! I don't know why they wouldn't let me go in to look for you.

I told Jeff they had you disguised in bandages like—Dame May Whitty was her name! In *The Lady Vanishes*."

"Help me!" calls Ilka.

"Mom, I'm going to take you home, only they may want to keep you awhile for observation, okay?" Maggie is distracted by trying not to turn around to look at the naked old woman on the recliner across from the nurses' station. "Hang on," Maggie says to her mother, and she gets up and walks over to a nurse who is typing at a computer station. "Excuse me, but that woman has taken off her gown."

The nurse says, "Is that so," and goes on typing.

"Maggie!" calls Ilka.

"Coming." Maggie picks up the blanket off the floor and hands it to the old naked woman, who throws it onto the floor.

"Isn't it odd," says Maggie, sitting down by her mother, "that what we're ashamed of and hide from each other are the things we have in common, like peeing, and what we pee with?"

"Help me!" calls Ilka.

"Mom?"

"Maggie!" calls Ilka.

"Darling, I'm here," says Maggie.

"Help me!" calls Ilka. "Maggie!"

"Mom, I'm right here. I'm here with you. Mom?" but Maggie is speaking out of our common world from which no sound, no sign, no kiss, or touch of the hand reaches into the nightmare in which Ilka Weiss is alone with her terror.

"Maggie!" she calls. "Help me!"

Maggie looks around, looks for help, sees the naked old woman on the recliner, sees the nurse typing.

"Maggie!"

Now the ice age, presaged by the worm under her ribs, settles into Maggie's chest. She thinks that she has crossed into another era from which she will look back with nostalgia to her life and to the things as they have been. Maggie is mistaken. The ice age in her chest will become the way that things are. Maggie sees Jeff talking to the nurse, who has stopped typing. She is pointing: It's all right, it turns out, for little David and baby Steven to visit their grandmother in the solarium.

V
The Meeting

Benedict goes to find Room 706 to tell Joe that Salman Haddad has rescheduled the meeting. "They're clearing a room for us on the seventh floor because you and my mom are already up here anyway. Al and I are supposed to report on our interviewees, Gorewitz and Rhinelander, who, incidentally, was sent home and has checked himself back in. Haddad wants Dr. Stimson—he's the head of Emergency—to go over his log of the sixty-two-pluses they've transferred to the seventh floor."

Among those in Dr. Stimson's log are: Ilka Weiss and Lilly Cobbler, who have been translated into a gap in the world where nobody can reach them; a note says that Cobbler's sister, Sadie Woodway, returned to the location of their former business on 57th Street and jumped to her death; the nonagenarian, Anstiss Adams, started beating her caretaker, Luba; Luba keeps taking her clothes off; Francis Rhinelander believes himself to be living in a musical; Samson Gorewitz thinks he is dead; and each of his sisters, Deborah and Shirley, who can't stop arguing; and Jack in his wheelchair, who cannot stop weeping.

"And, the reports, of course," says Benedict, "on you and my mom."

"It's the terrorists," says Joe.

"It's the Farkasz case, Haddad says, that muddies the issue. All the others walked into the ER with their minds apparently intact, and proceeded to go around the bend. Ida Farkasz was brought in with a diagnosis of retrograde amnesia, fell asleep on one of the chairs in the ER, and woke with her memory of a lifetime of rejection and humiliation perfectly restored. The hospital sent for her daughter to take her home. Phyllis from the second floor is sending Bethy to do a follow-up interview."

Joe says, "What interests me is that all our vitals are all good! The terrorists' problem is two-pronged: They have to drive us insane, while they keep us indefinitely alive. We are dealing with an enemy of enormous sophistication, ingenuity, and patience. They are able to imagine a West entirely populated by demented, heart-healthy centenarians."

"So okay," says Benedict, "so I'll go brief my mom."

Lucy and Jenny

When push comes to shove, the Senior Center cannot put boys and girls in the same room, even the ones that have been legally married these five-and-forty years.

Benedict finds his mother and Joe's wife, Jenny, in Room 712. He briefs Lucy about the revised plan for the meeting. "What," he asks Jenny Bernstine, "are *you* doing here?"

"I've gone around the bend," says Jenny. "I told that

lovely young doctor about so many things in my old age that I enjoy and she sent me to the seventh floor."

"What do you mean, things you enjoy? What 'things'?"

Jenny says, "I always think of the painting by Miró, at the Met. The card next to it quoted him saying, 'I confess that I look at real things with increasing love' and you know what things? 'the fuel lamp, potatoes.' Things," Jenny says, "and the holes they make in the fence so I can see the new building going up. The doggy bag. A mother and a baby smiling at each other and the cabbie who understands about little boys and their bears. My neighbor putting a quarter in the meter to save a stranger getting a ticket. Walking on Madison Avenue, my bed, my own apartment. I love Joe, I love my Beth, and I love it when they've gone to the office and I have my own kingdom all to myself." Jenny smiles. She is embarrassed. "I mean I like washing up the breakfast dishes with the sink filled full of sunlight. Moses had to strike a rock to water Israel, but a turn of my wrist and water flows cold, it flows hot. I flip a switch and there is light! I come out of my kitchen and if I stop in this particular spot I can see into my living room where I've arranged two armchairs as if there were friends on their way over. Lucy coming over, having a martini and sitting, talking!" Jenny says. "They've diagnosed me with bipolar depression stuck in a phase of permanent euphoria."

It's also true that Jenny wishes Lucy would put her glasses and cell phone away in her handbag, would stop scrabbling around in her PATIENTS PROPERTY bag.

What is Lucy looking for?

"Got it," says Lucy. "I've written a new story for Maurie to neither accept nor reject nor so much as acknowledge receipt of. It's about Sadie, the suicide."

"Oh, oh!" Jenny says. "I try to imagine what must have gone on in her head, her heart, in the hours before she jumped."

"In my story," Lucy says, "she has already jumped and gone to heaven, which nobody is good at imagining, unless you like Hallmark cloudscapes. Bunyan carries on about the gold and silver currency of Vanity Fair, but *he* can't think of anything better to interior-decorate *his* heaven with. Dante's crags and valleys remind me too much of the Hudson school of American painting so I confine myself to sheer numbers—the centuries of additional mortalities since Dante marveled at death having undone so many—I mean death's vastness. I'll read it to you. It's called 'Sadie in Heaven'—of course, I'll have to change the proper names."

Benedict says, "Mom, listen, I'll let you know when they decide the date of the meeting. Bye. Bye, Jenny."

Lucy reads her story to Jenny.

" *'Men have died from time to time,' says Shakespeare, 'and worms have eaten them,' but Sadie Woodway has passed, passed on, alternatively over, into heaven. She was a good woman. Sadie found satisfaction, even entertainment, in her daily work, and tenderly cared for her sister Lilly.*

"*Sadie misses Lilly. She looks around at the vast crowd of the dead who stand or move, as crowds will, in groups, singly, or in pairs. Such a number of children!*

"Lilly—the real Lilly, not the one who sits in the wheelchair with her mouth hanging open—Lilly would have remembered the name of the woman whom Sadie pretends not to notice. Sadie knows that she knows the woman but cannot for the death of her remember if this was a customer from their dressmaking business, or someone, maybe, from the old Chicago neighborhood? Might she be one of the Seattle aunts who has passed on?

"Sadie recognizes that white woman—Lilly would remember her name—the woman with the velvet pincushion strapped to her left wrist. She had hired Lilly and Sadie in Lord and Taylor's alterations department, a windowless room, dresses on hangers, dress forms, one big, one small, a treadle sewing machine, an ironing board, colored threads, stuffs—their first New York job. How old the old white woman looks! She can't see or doesn't remember Sadie. She would remember Lilly.

"Sadie could have known that neat young fellow if he'd been sitting where he belonged, behind the teller's window at the bank in which Sadie had deposited their weekly intake. He's out of context, in heaven, and she knows only that she knows him.

"Here comes a stout, laughing woman who embraces Sadie, welcomes her warmly, very kindly. Sadie cannot remember having ever laid eyes on her in all her born days and yet the woman asks after Lilly, after their brother, Clem. Says, 'You and Lilly came to my Jackie's wedding!' Sadie can tell that the woman can tell that this rings no bell for Sadie. The woman laughs, which is good-natured of her. 'Not to worry! It happens to all of us!' she says, and here comes the old customer, neighbor, or aunt, whose name Sadie cannot remember, and whom, if she weren't dead, she would die of embarrassment to not be able to introduce to the woman she doesn't remember having ever met before.

"After this Sadie looks for a place out of the traffic. How thankful she would be for the smallest little cloud that she could sit down behind and stay hidden while she waits for Lilly to join her."

"Poor Sadie," concludes Lucy. "She will wait a long, long time if Joe's theory is right and the terrorists are driving us insane while they simultaneously cure our fatal illnesses, to stop us from dying unless, like Sadie, we take our escape into our own hands." What Lucy is waiting for is for Jenny to say that "Sadie in Heaven" is a funny and marvelous story.

"Poor, poor, poor Sadie," says Jenny.

Benedict has come to say that they must put off the meeting till Joe feels better. Joe's vitals are not good. He lies on his side, his cheek in his wife's palm, grins palely, and says, "Anatomize my Jenny. Is there any cause in nature that breeds these good hearts?"

The delay gives Phyllis time to arrange Bethy's follow-up visit to Ida Farkasz.

Ida and the Crazy Box

Bethy is knocking on the door of apartment 3A when the downstairs neighbor's head appears at the top of the stairs. "If you're looking for Mrs. Farkasz, she's gone."

"Gone? Gone where? Where have they taken her, and why haven't we been informed?"

"No one has taken her. She's gone back to Santo Domingo." Sophie Bauer introduces herself. "You want to come in and have a cup of coffee? Marta—that's her daughter—came and helped her pack, and Poldi, the sister, was here to say good-bye. Ida's gone back to the hotel that used to be run by a Polish couple or Czech or Hungarian—I forget—where they lived before they came to New York and you could get a girl to do for you for like eight dollars a month."

"But does she have family over there?"

"*No!* That's why she went! Where she won't have to be keeping Poldi from coming around, she said, or sit on a chair in her apartment without even a window to see what's going on in the street outside, waiting for the daughter to not visit and to not even return her phone call!"

"But you can sit and wait and not get a phone call in Santo Domingo."

"You can, I know you can, but you know, you don't. I don't know why, but I'm sad—I feel terrible when my daughter, Sally, in Queens doesn't give me a call, but I don't expect my youngest to call me from Albuquerque. You don't sit and wait for people to call you long distance, you just don't."

"That's funny. That's true," says Beth. "You know what Ida Farkasz is sitting in her room in the hotel waiting for? Her daughter to not write to her."

"That's what she is sitting doing, you're right!" says Sophie Bauer. "The poor thing is waiting to not get a letter. What she needs is to get her amnesia back."

But Sophie and Bethy are mistaken. Ida has had a letter from Marta. She holds it on her lap. She sits on a chair in her rented room in what used to be the Hotel Budapest grown dingy and in need of repairs. It is sixty years since Ida, Miklos, and the baby had the room now occupied by the new owner, a Dominican who has renamed the Hotel Malecón.

Marta wrote, "If you want to see Poldi you need to invite her, and soon. You know she isn't well, Mama, and the rest are all gone, Papa, Onkel Kari, your sister Berta. What they did or didn't do is two wars, an emigration, and a Holocaust ago!"

Ida sits. She stares out the window. She does not see the little green-and-golden bird insert its needle beak into the hibiscus blossom's rude red trumpet. The bird stands in midair by action of its wings, which create a phantom wheel like a plane's propeller that has reached its full speed. The bird extracts the last drop of sweet nourishment from the red bloom outside Ida's window and flies away. In the crazy box Ida watches Berta—Berta whose face was the loveliest always, even at near three hundred pounds when it was a project to just get her up from her chair. Berta is running. She runs left, has to turn at the shout of a uniformed boy with a gun, and runs right. The boy shouts at Berta, who cannot run, to keep running.

"Mama!" wrote Marta. "Whatever Berta did, what they all did—Poldi, Papa, Uncle Herbie, forget it, Mama! Mama, let it go!"

Let it go? Forget it? Forget the anti-Semites at Kastel Street not telling Ida—or Herbie—that there were courses they needed to take? Forget the thirty-five dollars Herbie made her pay for the bedcover that *she* had sewed for him? *One lousy postcard!* Miklos with Berta's carpet under his arm. Poldi blocking Miss Margate's front door to keep Ida from coming in. Poldi who had gone to Herta's birthday. Marta who didn't bother to put a comb to her hair when she came to help with the packing …

Ida knows that she can let it go! Ida can let everything go, all of it. She feels a chill, like a north wind blowing through the room in the Hotel Malecón. She looks out the window at an alien lifescape, and Ida grapples them to her for warmth, for company, for something to think about—the old familiars, her treasury of resentments.

Had Ida been a real witch, what power she would have drawn from the cache of her grudges—what meanness she could have done if she had somebody to be mean to.

Bethy

The meeting is scheduled for eleven o'clock, and Bethy grabs a cab to get to the cafeteria ahead of the others. This time she is going to seat herself where she won't have Al Lesser's shoulder in her face. Benedict, who has a way of leaning forward on his elbows, always blocks her view of what is going on at whichever end of the table her father is sitting. Now that Joe is not going to be attending any meeting—they've had to move him down to the third floor—it's for Bethy to stage-manage which end will be the head of the table and to seat herself at it. It's already five after; she's lucky to be the first to arrive. Bethy sets out her Farkasz notes on a table—she doesn't know that it's the table Lucy had bagged—of a size to accommodate the four remaining Compendium people, Lucy, Benedict, Al, and Bethy herself; the two Haddads, Dr. Miriam and Salman; and Dr. Stimson. Bethy is not sure whether she has ever met him.

11:15. After coffee and a doughnut, Bethy has another doughnut. At 11:20 she understands that nobody is coming. Is it possible that they've reverted to the original plan of meeting in Salman Haddad's office and nobody has bothered to tell her? Why are people not answering their phones? And now Bethy is helplessly late, grabs up the Farkasz report which slips out of her hands, launches itself upon the air and fans across the floor, nor is there time to collate the pages. Bethy runs for the elevator, which takes her down to the atrium level. She sprints through the Sydney and Sylvia B. Holloway Building and turns right to the Seymour D. and Vivian L. Levi Pavilion. It shocks Bethy that her urgency has no effect whatever on the preordained speed at which the elevator ascends. The doors take their time to open and let out the two merciless passengers; they are not in any hurry. The orderly has to wait to wheel in the empty hospital bed that he is taking up to the next floor where it refuses to budge until he can resolve the problem with the locking mechanism.

It takes Bethy several nightmare minutes to understand that she is not going to find the door to Haddad's office because she has come up the wrong elevators in the wrong building. Briefly she sobs. Bethy waits for the elevator that will take her back down to the atrium level, where she sprints through the Seymour D. and Vivian L. Levi Pavilion, turns left through the Sydney and Sylvia B. Holloway Building, and locates the bank of elevators that take her up to the security offices.

Secretaries hate Bethy Bernstine. The large blonde who runs Salman Haddad's office had been short with Bethy that first time, when they'd come to get their social-worker identities and been told to find Phyllis on the second floor. Today the tone of the secretary's voice suggests that her work contract does not include, nor is she being adequately compensated for, informing Bethy that the meeting is at this moment going forward in a room set aside for the purpose on the seventh floor of the Senior Center.

The meeting is indeed going forward but the only persons present are Benedict, Al Lesser, and an intern sent by Dr. Stimson to say that he is with a patient on the third floor, that he will be detained, and to start the meeting without him.

The intern's name is Tola (she is one of the interns with the flapping white coats and the faces of people who have the stamina for years of study, who were laughing as they crossed the atrium in which the Compendium people waited to meet Dr. Miriam Haddad). Tola is young, brilliant, and on a crusade against the hospital's stultification and mismanagement. Dr. Stimson, she has been telling Al and Benedict, is of the old reverence-for-life-at-all-costs mentality. "The world outside the hospital," says Tola in the enthusiasm of her young bitterness, "has no concept that the things we do to keep the patient alive another day, another twelve hours, meet Abu Ghraib standards." The interns have drawn up a heroic declaration, which might be as much as their careers are worth, to challenge the old guard's superannuated misreading of what the Hippocratic oath intends by "doing no harm." They are collecting signatures and Tola has brought a copy with her. Benedict and Al add their signatures and e-mail addresses so they can be informed of any action in which they might join the embattled interns.

Where is everybody who is supposed to be at the meeting?

Bethy has run the several blocks up the sidewalk and is at this moment entering the Senior Center through its glass double doors. As she regains her breath going up the Sabbath Elevator, Bethy looks down the perspective of her future where she will never sit at the head, nor in the central position, at any table.

On the seventh floor, she gets out and meets Benedict and Al coming out of the room dedicated to the meeting which is not going to take place.

"Oops!" Benedict says, and he feels a little bit bad. "I guess I thought you were in the room—weren't you in Joe's room when I told him that the meeting had been rescheduled on the seventh floor?"

Joe Bernstine has been transferred to a room on the third floor where he lies in a hospital bed with his right hand taped to to his side. Dr. Stimson tells the nurse, "I want him sitting up. And remove the tape."

"He keeps fiddling with the intubation," says the nurse.

"I'll take care of it."

The nurse raises the back of the bed to a sitting position and frees Joe's hand. Joe lifts it to the tube, which chafes the sore right corner of his mouth. The doctor, who has seated himself on the edge of the bed, takes Joe's hand. He regards the sick man who regards him from under half-closed lids.

Dr. Stimson says, "We know you can't talk with the tube down your throat. It's uncomfortable."

Joe closes his lids all the way and opens them.

"You see, you can blink 'yes.' Tell me 'yes' again. Keep your eyes closed for a moment so that we both know that you mean 'yes.' "

Joe shuts his eyes all the way and keeps them shut for a two-count.

"Good. That's right. That's good. We know you would feel a whole lot better if we could take the breathing tube out."

Joe blinks a two-count "Yes."

"If I remove the tube from your throat there is a probability—not a certainty, but a high probability—that you will not be able to breathe on your own. You understand that. Yes?"

Joe takes a moment. He blinks. He understands that.

"Okay, let me state this as a fact: If I remove the tube I would not—I can*not*—reinsert it. Do you understand?"

Why would Joe not take a long moment to think about this? He blinks. He understands this also.

The doctor holds Joe's hand in his hand. "Do you wish me to remove the breathing tube? Take your time."

Joe takes his time. He takes such a very long time that the doctor says, "I'm going to put it to you the other way around, so we can be very very clear that we know what you want me to do, and so we don't have to put you through this conversation again: Do you wish me to leave the tube in?"

Joe is still taking his time, thinking. His eyes do not lower their lids, neither with the rapid natural blink that moistens the eyeball, nor with the two-count blink that means yes and chooses life over death, or chooses death over life.

The doctor sits on the edge of the bed with Joe's hand in his hand. He regards his patient. Joe regards the doctor.

Lucy sits in the solarium. If you find, reader, that you are tired of Lucy looking for her glasses, think how tiresome it is for *her* to find them and have to hold a finger in the page of the address book while she takes the cell phone out of its niche. There aren't enough hands to remove the glasses from their case and, having identified the talk button on the cell, put them on her nose so that she can check the number that she has never been able to hold in her head long enough to dial.

"Kathy? I don't believe this! I never expect you to pick up! I call, and there you are at the other end of the line! I want to read you my funny short-short about being dead."

Katherine says she is burning to hear Lucy's story. Lucy reads Katherine "Sadie in Heaven." Katherine's detailed, specific, accurate, high praise is what Lucy has been waiting her life long to hear, does not believe, and experiences as an act of hostility.

Because Lucy is wearing her readers, her reflection in the night-black glass of the solarium wall is blurred. A blurred nurse wheels in a recliner on which the blurry old Luba lies naked; they've given up trying to get her to keep covered. And here they come, all the sixty-two-pluses who have gone around the bend, naked every last one. Here comes that sweet old Rhinelander, his elongated limbs have the wavy articulation of an El Greco saint seen from the worm's-eye view. The naked nonagenarian, Anstiss, has elegant bones, a noble skull. Here's Samson, the drowned fat man from Glenshore's night beach. His belly is the familiar kind that starts under his breasts. The crying old Jack looks peculiarly naked because his large, dark, hairy head looks dressed. Naked Hope with her gray locks open about her shoulders pushes his chair. One nurse leads old, lost Ilka by the arm, and another wheels in the huge black Lilly who overflows her chair. The

Gorewitz sisters walk with their heads turned to each other like the talking profiles in old *New Yorker* cocktail party cartoons. This is the party of the unaccommodated, the men one penis apiece, the women each with her two dugs. Lucy observes herself reaching behind herself to undo the tie at the back of her neck, and the one behind her waist.

Dr. Miriam Haddad, who knows she is late for the meeting in the Senior Center, passes the open door of Cedars of Lebanon's Interdenominational Chapel. Correction: The chapel *has* no door. The chapel stands open at all times to all. Miriam looks in and calls Salman on her cell.

Salman is walking out of the door of his office when his secretary calls him back. "Your wife wants you down in the chapel, right away."

"What for? Hand me the phone?"

"She's hung up. She said, right away."

"Where *is* this chapel?"

"Next to Cedars of Lebanon's Chase Bank branch office."

"What's up?" Salman asks Miriam. "We're late for the meeting."

"Look!"

Standing in the doorless opening, Salman Haddad looks at the potted palm, the standing lamp, the neutral space dedicated to welcoming anybody's faith and offending nobody's taste. Salman sees the pink soles of the kneeling man whose forehead touches the ground. A kneeling child with ecstatically upraised arms is not, on closer look, a child but a small little woman in a little dress wearing Mary Janes with lace-trimmed white socks. An old man under a prayer shawl is davening.

"Miriam, *what*? What did I hurry down here for?"

"Look on the wall, across from the standing lamp. You took your time, and it's already fading!"

When questioned, the three worshippers agree that they saw a moving finger doing graffiti on the wall. What do they think it wrote? "The Lord Is One," or "Kyrie Eleison"? It means that it is now theoretically possible to live forever. Dr. Miriam Haddad thinks that what the finger has written is "Sorry!" with an exclamation point. Salman Haddad walks over and makes out that the fast fading letters spell "Oops!" Miriam is right about the exclamation point.

In the room on the third floor, Dr. Stimson sits and waits on the edge of the bed in which Joe Bernstine lies supported by pillows and probably cannot breathe without the tube in his throat. The doctor is waiting for Joe to blink. And if they haven't died, as the story says, they are living to this hour.

Acknowledgments

I would like to thank friends who have read, thought about, and told me what they thought about *Half the Kingdom*, through its several changes: Allen Bergson, Deirdre Bergson, Alan Friedman, Vivian Gornick, Joyce Johnson, Gene Lichtenstein, James Marcus, Norma Rosen, Barry Schechter, Matthew Sharpe. I thank David Segal for the research I never feel like doing myself, and Angelo Pastormerlo for suggesting certain books for Joe Bernstine's library. Thank you, Kathy Earnest, for lending me the character of Mrs. West, the piano teacher. I want to thank Dr. Eric Cassel and Dr. Flavia Golden for conversations about the procedures in emergency rooms. They are not responsible for the outcomes.

I thank the Cullman Center for Writers and Scholars for the good year in which I wrote portions of the book.

Parts of this book were published, in somewhat different form, in *Harper's Magazine* (May 2011) and in *The New Yorker* (December 24, 2007).